The Shore Road Mystery
"WE'LL TIE THEM UP UNTIL WE FIGURE OUT WHAT TO DO WITH
THEM."

THE SHORE ROAD
MYSTERY

By
FRANKLIN W. DIXON

First Published 1928
Republished 2024

CHAPTER

I	Stolen Cars
II	Circumstantial Evidence
III	Under Suspicion
IV	Out on Bail
V	More Thieving
VI	On the Shore Road
VII	Gus Montrose
VIII	The Missing Truck
IX	Following Clues
X	The Great Discovery
XI	Fish
XII	The New Car
XIII	In the Locker
XIV	Montrose Again
XV	The Suspect
XVI	Kidnaped
XVII	The Cave
XVIII	The Auto Thieves
XIX	Captured
XX	Tables Turned
XXI	At the Farmhouse
XXII	The Round-Up
XXIII	The Mystery Solved

CHAPTER I
Stolen Cars

"It certainly is a mystery how those autos disappeared," said Frank Hardy.

"I'll say it is," replied his brother Joe, raising his voice to be heard above the clatter of their motorcycles. "Just think of it! Two cars last week, two the week before, and one the week before that. Some thieving, I'll tell the world."

"And Martin's car was brand new," called back Chet Morton.

"Mighty tough," Frank affirmed. "It's bad enough to lose a car, but to have it stolen the day after you've bought it is a little too much."

"Must be a regular gang of car thieves at work."

The three boys, on their motorcycles, were speeding along the Shore Road that skirted Barmet Bay, just out of Bayport, on a sunny Saturday afternoon.

"A person takes a big risk leaving a car parked along this road," said Chet. "Every one of the five autos disappeared along the shore."

"What beats me," declared Frank, turning out to avoid a mud puddle, "is how the thieves got away with them. None of them were seen coming into Bayport and there was no trace of them at the other end of the Shore Road, either. Seems as if they just vanished into the thin air."

Chet slowed down so that the trio were riding abreast.

"If the cars were only ordinary flivvers it wouldn't be so bad. But they were all expensive, high-powered hacks. Martin's car would be spotted anywhere, and so would the others. It's funny that no one saw them."

"Some of these auto thieves are mighty smart," opined Joe. "They certainly have their nerve, working this road for three weeks, and with everybody on the lookout for them. It has certainly put a crimp in the bathing and fishing along the Shore Road." He gestured toward the beach below. "Why, usually on a Saturday afternoon like this you'll see a dozen cars parked along here. What with boating and fishing and swimming, lots of people used to come out from town. Now, if they come at all, they walk."

"And you can't blame 'em. Who wants to lose a high-priced car just for the sake of an hour's fishing?"

"It's certainly mighty strange," Frank reiterated. "After taking two cars from almost the same place, you'd imagine the thieves would be scared to come back."

"They have plenty of nerve, that's certain."

"It isn't as if the police haven't been busy. They've watched this road ever since the first car was lost, and the other autos were stolen just the same. They've kept an eye on both ends of the highway and there wasn't a sign of any of them."

"It's strange that they haven't turned up somewhere. Lots of times a stolen car will be recovered when the thief tries to get rid of it. The engine numbers alone often trip them up. Of course, I guess they'd clap on false license plates, but it's pretty hard to get away with a fine-looking car like Martin's unless it's been repainted and altered a bit."

"It's no fun to lose a car," declared Chet. "I remember how badly I felt when the crooks stole my roadster last year."

"You got it back, anyway."

"Yes, I got it back. But I was mighty blue until I did."

The motorcycles rounded a bend in the road and before the boys lay a wide stretch of open highway, descending in a gradual slope. To their right lay Barmet Bay, sparkling in the afternoon sun. At the bottom of the slope was a grassy expanse that opened out on the beach, the road at this point being only a few feet above the sea level. The little meadow was a favorite parking place for motorists, as their cars could regain the road easily, but to-day there was not an automobile in sight.

"Look at that," said Frank. "No one here on a nice afternoon like this."

At that moment, however, the appearance of a man who came running up from the beach and across the grass, belied his words.

"Some one's here all right," remarked Joe. "And he seems in a hurry about something."

As the boys rode down the slope they could see the man hastening out into the middle of the road, where he stood waving his arms.

"Looks like Isaac Fussy, doesn't it?" said Chet.

"The rich old fisherman?"

"Yes, it's Fussy all right. Look at him dancing around. Wonder what's the matter."

In a few moments the boys had drawn near enough to see that the old man who was waving at them so frantically was indeed the wealthy and eccentric old fisherman known as Isaac Fussy. He was a queer old fellow who lived by himself in a big house on the outskirts of Bayport, and who spent much of his time on the bay. Just now he was evidently in a state of great agitation, shouting and waving his arms as the boys approached.

The motorcycles came to a stop.

"Anything wrong?" asked Frank.

"After 'em! After 'em!" shouted the old man, his face crimson with wrath, as he shook his fist in the air. "Chase 'em, lads!"

"Who? What's the matter, Mr. Fussy?"

"Thieves! That's what's the matter! My automobile!"

"Stolen?"

"Stolen! Robbed! I left it here not ten minutes ago and was startin' out in my boat to fish. I just looked back in time to see somebody drivin' away in it. An outrage!" shouted Mr. Fussy. "After 'em!"

"Why, it's been stolen just a few minutes ago, then?"

"They just went tearin' around the bend before you came in sight. If you look lively, you'll catch 'em. You know my car—it's a big blue Cadillac sedan. Paid twenty-eight hundred for it. Catch them thieves and I'll reward you. Don't waste time standin' here talkin' about it—"

The motorcycles roared and leaped forward.

"We'll do our best!" shouted Frank, as he crouched low over the handle bars.

A cloud of dust arose as the three powerful machines sped off down the road, leaving Isaac Fussy still muttering imprecations on the thieves who had stolen his Cadillac.

The boys were excited and elated. This was as close as any one had yet come to being on the trail of the auto thieves, and they knew that in their fast motorcycles they possessed a decided advantage. If, as Isaac Fussy said, the car had just disappeared around the bend a few minutes previously, they stood an excellent chance of overtaking it.

The motorcycles slanted far over to the side as they took the curve in a blinding screen of dust, then righted again as they sped down the next open stretch at terrific speed. There was no sign of the stolen car, but the open stretch was only about a quarter of a mile in length, skirting the shore, and the road then wound inland behind a bank of trees.

The clamor of the pounding motors filled the summer air as the boys raced in pursuit. Before them was a thin haze of dust, just settling in the road, which indicated that an automobile had passed that way only a few minutes before. "We'll catch 'em!" shouted Chet, jubilantly.

Without slackening speed, they took the next curve and then found themselves speeding through a cool grove, where the road wound about, cutting off the view ahead. When at length they emerged into an open section of farming land they gazed anxiously into the distance in hope of seeing their quarry, but they were disappointed. The fleeing car was not yet in sight.

Down the road, between the crooked fences, they raced, the engines raising a tremendous racket.

A few hundred yards ahead was the entrance to a lane that led into a farm. The lane was lined with dense trees.

Suddenly, Frank gasped and desperately began to cut down his speed. For, out of this lane, emerged a team of horses, drawing a huge wagonload of hay.

The dust raised by Frank's motorcycle obscured the view of the other boys, and for a moment they did not realize what was happening. The trees along the lane had hidden the hay wagon from sight and Frank was almost upon it before he realized the danger. It was impossible to stop in time.

The man on the hay wagon shouted and waved his arms. The horses reared. The clumsy vehicle presented a barrier directly across the road.

There was only one thing for it. The boys had to take to the ditch to avoid a collision. There was no time to stop.

Frank wheeled his speeding machine to the left, praying for the best. For a moment, he thought he would make it. The motorcycle bumped and lurched, and then it went over on its side and he was flung violently over the handle bars into the bushes ahead.

Behind him he heard shouts, the roar of the other machines, and then two crashes, which came almost simultaneously. Chet and Joe had also been spilled.

CHAPTER II

Circumstantial Evidence

For a moment Frank Hardy lay in the thicket, stunned by the shock of his fall, with the breath knocked out of him. Gradually, he recovered himself and managed to scramble to his feet. His first thought was for the other boys, but a quick glance showed that both Chet and Joe were unhurt, beyond a few bruises.

Joe was sitting in the ditch, looking around him in bewilderment, as though he had not yet realized exactly what had happened, while Chet Morton was picking himself up out of a clump of undergrowth near the fence. In the road, the driver of the hay wagon was trying to calm his startled horses, who were rearing and plunging in fright.

"Any bones broken?" asked Frank of his two companions.

Chet carefully counted his ribs.

"Guess not," he announced, cheerfully. "I think I'm all here, safe and sound. Wow! What a spill that was!"

Joe got to his feet.

"Good thing this is a soft ditch," he said. "It's lucky somebody didn't get a broken neck."

"Well, nobody did, and that's that. How about the bikes?"

Frank examined his own motorcycle, righted it, and found that the machine was not damaged beyond a bent mudguard. He had managed to slow down sufficiently before careering into the ditch, so that much of the shock had been averted and the motorcycle had simply turned over into the spongy turf.

"My bike's all right," announced Chet. "It's bent a little here and there, but it's good for a few more miles yet."

"Same here," said Joe Hardy, looking up. "I think we're mighty lucky to get off so easily."

"You mighta run me down!" roared the driver of the hay wagon, now that he had recovered from his fright. "Tearin' and snortin' down the road on them contraptions—"

"Why don't you watch the road?" asked Frank. "You heard us coming. We couldn't see you. You might have killed the three of us, driving out like that. You didn't have anything to worry about."

"I didn't, eh?"

"No."

"What if I'd been killed?"

"You could hear our bikes half a mile off—unless you are deaf," put in Joe.

"It ain't my business to listen for them contraptions," growled the man on the hay wagon. "I got my work to do."

"Well, don't blame us," said Frank. "And the next time you drive out of a side road like that, stop, look and listen."

"Say, who do you think you're givin' orders to?" and now the man reached for his whip and acted as if he meant to get down and thrash somebody.

"None of that—if you know when you are well off," cried Joe, his eyes blazing.

Chet stepped forward.

"If you say the word, we'll give you all that is coming to you," he put in.

All of the boys looked so determined that the man let his whip alone.

"Get out o' my way! I got to be goin'," he growled.

"Well, after this you be more careful," said Frank.

The driver grumbled, but the boys were not disposed to remain and argue the rights and wrongs of the matter. It had been an accident, pure and simple, with a certain amount of blame on both sides, so they mounted their motorcycles and drove on. Because of the spill, the boys realized that their chances of overtaking the car thieves were correspondingly lessened, but they decided to continue the pursuit. "At the rate they're going," said Chet, hopefully, "they may have an upset themselves."

While the Hardy boys and their chum are speeding along the Shore Road on the trail of the stolen sedan, it will not be out of place to introduce them more fully to new readers.

Frank and Joe Hardy were the sons of Fenton Hardy, a famous detective who had made a national reputation for himself while on the detective force of the New York Police Department and who had retired to set up a private practice of his own. Frank Hardy was a tall, dark lad, sixteen years old, while his brother Joe was a fair, curly-headed chap, a year younger. Both boys were students at the high school in Bayport.

When Fenton Hardy retired from the metropolitan force, owing to the great demand for his services in private investigations, he had moved with his family to Bayport, a thriving city of fifty thousand, on Barmet Bay, on the Atlantic seaboard. Here the two boys attended school and here it was that they met with the first adventures that strengthened their resolution to follow in their father's footsteps and themselves become detectives when they grew older.

Fenton Hardy was one of the greatest American criminologists, and his sons had inherited much of his ability. From their earliest boyhood it had been their united ambition to be detectives but in this they had been discouraged by their parents, who preferred to see them inclined toward medicine or the bar. However, these professions held little attraction for the lads, and when they eventually had an opportunity to display their ability as amateur detectives they felt that they had scored a point toward realizing their ambition.

In the first volume of this series, "The Hardy Boys: The Tower Treasure," the lads cleared up a mystery centering about a strange mansion on the outskirts of Bayport, recovering a quantity of stolen jewelry and bonds after the police and even Fenton Hardy had been forced to admit themselves baffled. Thereafter, their father had made but mild objections to the pursuit of their hobby and was, indeed, secretly proud of the ability displayed by his sons. Further mysteries were solved by the boys, the stories of which have been recounted in previous volumes of this series, the preceding book, "Hunting for Hidden Gold," relating their adventures in the far West, where they faced a bandit gang and went after a fortune in hidden gold in the depths of an abandoned mine.

Chet Morton, who was with the Hardy boys this afternoon, was one of their high school chums, a plump, good-natured lad with a weakness for food "and lots of it," as he frequently said. He lived on a farm about a mile outside Bayport and, like the Hardy boys, was the proud owner of a motorcycle. Frank and Joe also owned a motorboat, the *Sleuth*, which they had bought from the proceeds of a reward they had earned by their work in solving a mystery. Tony Prito, an Italian-American lad, and Biff Hooper, two other high school chums of the Hardy boys, also owned motorboats, in which the boys spent many happy hours on Barmet Bay and in which they had, incidentally, experienced a number of thrilling adventures.

"Often wished I owned a boat," said Chet, as they sped along, "but now I'm just as glad I have a motorcycle instead. I'd have missed all this fun this afternoon if I hadn't."

"You have a queer idea of fun," Joe remarked. "Getting dumped out on my head into a wet ditch doesn't make me laugh very hard."

"Better than studying algebra." Chet's aversion to school work was well known.

For a while they sped on without talking. There was no sign of the stolen automobile, but the boys did not entirely give up hope of catching up with it. When they had gone about three miles, however, even Frank was forced to admit that the fugitives had doubtless given them the slip.

"What's going on over there?" said Frank suddenly. "There's a state trooper and three men over in that farmyard."

"And a big car, too," said Chet.

"Why, I know this place," Joe declared. "This is Dodd's farm."

"Not Jack Dodd? The chap who goes to Bayport High."

"Sure. This is where he lives. I remember the place was pointed out to me once."

"I knew Jack Dodd lived on a farm but I didn't know it was this far out," said Chet. "Let's drop in and see what's up."

With Frank in the lead the three boys turned down the lane leading in to the Dodd place.

"I wonder what that trooper is here for," he said. "They all seem to be having an argument over something."

"Perhaps the trooper met the auto thieves!" conjectured Chet.

When they drove into the barnyard they saw a boy running toward them and they recognized him as Jack Dodd, a quiet, likable lad who was in their class at the Bayport high school.

"Hello, fellows!" he called to them, but they saw that there was a worried expression on his face. "What brings you away out here to-day?"

"Hunting trip," said Chet, with a curious glance toward the state trooper, who was standing over by the fence with Mr. Dodd and two burly strangers. Their voices were raised in a loud argument, in which Mr. Dodd appeared to be opposed to the others.

"Hunting trip?"

"Hunting for auto thieves," Frank explained. "Isaac Fussy's car was stolen a little while ago. When we saw that trooper here we had an idea that perhaps he might know something about it."

"What's that?" shouted the trooper, a broad-shouldered young chap. "A car stolen?"

"Yes, sir. We were chasing it. A big Cadillac."

"Didn't see it," replied the trooper. "It didn't pass this way, I'm sure of that. We've just found one stolen car, anyway."

"I tell you I didn't steal it!" declared Mr. Dodd heatedly. "I haven't the least idea how that car got there."

"That's all right," interposed one of the other men gruffly. "You can tell that to the judge. The fact is, we've found the car behind your barn and it's one of the cars that were stolen in the past couple of weeks."

The chums glanced questioningly at Jack Dodd.

"These men are detectives," he said, in a low voice. "They came out from the city with the trooper a little while ago."

"Did they really find a stolen car here?" asked Chet.

Jack nodded.

"They found one all right, but how on earth it got here, I don't know. It's a Packard and somebody must have driven it in and left it among the bushes behind the barn. We never noticed it."

"Well," the state trooper was saying, "I'm going to drive the car back to Bayport and return it to the owner. You don't claim it's yours, do you?" He gestured toward a splendid touring car near by.

"Of course it isn't mine," said Mr. Dodd. "I've never seen it before and I never want to see it again—"

"I guess you don't," growled one of the detectives.

"How it got here, I can't tell. I certainly had nothing to do with stealing it."

"People don't leave perfectly good cars hidden behind other people's barns," said the other detective. "You'd better tell us a straight story, Dodd. It'll be easier for you."

"I've told you all I know about it."

"Well, then, if you don't know any more about it, perhaps your son does."

"I don't know any more than Dad," declared Jack stoutly. "I've never seen the car before."

"Never?"

"No."

One of the detectives stepped swiftly over to the automobile and produced an object from the back seat. He held it out toward the boy.

"What's this?" he asked.

Jack gasped.

"My fishing rod!"

"It's yours, is it? How did it get there if you've never seen the car before?"

CHAPTER III

Under Suspicion

For a moment after the detective's question there was dead silence. Jack Dodd stared at the fishing rod as though stupefied. Then, mechanically, he took it in his hands.

"Yes, it's mine, all right," he admitted. "I lost it."

"Oh, you lost it, did you?" said the detective unpleasantly. "That's very likely. You lost it in that car."

"I didn't! I've never seen the car. I left my fishing rod out by the front fence about a week ago and when I came to look for it the rod was gone."

The other detective snickered incredulously.

"It's true," protested Mr. Dodd. "Jack told me at the time that he had lost his rod."

"You'd back him up, of course. But that story won't go down. If he never saw the car before, how does his fishing rod happen to be in it?"

Jack and his father looked blankly at one another. Clearly, they were utterly astounded by this unexpected development, and at a loss to account for it.

"I think this pretty well clinches it," declared the trooper. "The rod couldn't have got there unless the boy was in the car—that's certain."

"But I wasn't in the car. I lost the rod a week ago."

"You'd say that, anyway," declared one of the detectives roughly. "Bring the car back to town, Jim." He turned to Mr. Dodd. "This isn't the end of the matter. There's not much doubt in my mind that you and your boy took that car. You certainly haven't been able to give us much of an explanation of how it came to be on your property, and the boy has told a pretty thin story to explain away that fishing rod."

"You're not going to arrest me!" exclaimed Mr. Dodd.

"No," said the detective reluctantly. "You don't have to come back with us. I guess you won't go very far away. But we're going to lay charges against you and your son."

"For what?"

"For stealing that car. What else do you think? And we're going to do a little more investigating about those other cars that were stolen, too."

Mr. Dodd said nothing. He realized the futility of objection. Nothing he might say would swerve the detectives from their determination to charge him and Jack with car stealing. On circumstantial evidence, they would be branded as thieves.

The state trooper turned to the Hardy boys and Chet, who had remained silent during this exchange of words.

"You boys said there was another car stolen?"

Frank nodded.

"A Cadillac sedan. It was stolen about half an hour ago, on the Shore Road."

"Describe it."

The trooper took out his notebook.

"We don't know the number. It was a blue sedan."

"Who did it belong to?"

"Isaac Fussy, the rich old fisherman."

"I've seen that car," said the trooper. "I'd recognize it anywhere. It didn't pass along this road. You've been following it?"

"We were right behind it until we had a spill a few miles back. That held us up for a while."

"I see. Well, the car has probably got away by a side road. I'll report it at headquarters, anyway."

He turned briskly away and went over to the Packard, getting into the front seat and taking his place at the wheel. The two detectives followed.

11

"You'll hear from us again in a day or so," said one gruffly to Mr. Dodd. "See that you stay here."

"I have nothing at all to fear. I didn't steal the car."

"You can tell that in court. Tell your boy to think up a better yarn about the fishing rod."

With this parting shot, the officers drove away.

Stunned by the misfortune that had befallen them, Mr. Dodd and Jack were silent. Frank Hardy was the first to speak.

"I'm sure it'll turn out all right, Jack. There's been a big mistake somewhere."

"Of course there's been a mistake," returned the boy heavily. "But it looks mighty bad for us."

"I've been living on this farm for more than thirty years," said Henry Dodd, "and there's never been any one could say anything against my good name or the name of any one in my family. I've no more idea how that automobile got here, than—" He shrugged his shoulders, and moved slowly away toward the house.

"We've told the truth," declared Jack. "We never saw the car before. We didn't know it was here. And I told them the truth about my fishing rod. I lost it last week and I didn't see it until that detective took it out of the automobile. How it got there, I don't know."

The chums were sympathetic. They tried, to the best of their ability, to cheer up Jack Dodd, although in their hearts they knew that the evidence against the boy would weigh heavily in a court of law.

"If you had known anything about the car and if you had left your fishing rod there you wouldn't have identified it so readily," said Frank shrewdly. "That was what made me certain you were telling the truth."

"I was so surprised at seeing the rod I couldn't help it! I told them just what they wanted to know. I suppose if I had lied about it they wouldn't have been so sure."

"It's always best to tell the truth in the long run," declared Frank. "It looks rather black for you just now, but after all they haven't very much to go on. The main thing is to find out who did hide that car behind the barn."

"And who put the fishing rod in it," added Joe Hardy.

"I don't suppose you suspect any one?"

Jack Dodd was thoughtful.

"I hadn't thought of it before," he said slowly; "but we had a hired man here up until last week who wouldn't be above playing a trick like that on us."

"Who was he?"

"His name was Gus Montrose. He worked here for about two months, but we had to let him go. He was lazy and he drank a lot and last week he had a quarrel with my father; so he was dismissed. I wouldn't say he stole the car and left it here, but he's the only person I can think of who might have cause to do anything like that."

"He might have had something to do with the fishing rod, at any rate," said Chet.

"He was a surly, bad-tempered fellow, and when he left he swore that he'd get even with us. But of course that may have been only talk."

"Talk or no talk, it's something to work on," Frank Hardy remarked. "Have you seen him around since?"

Jack shook his head.

"Haven't seen or heard of him."

"It's rather suspicious, having a thing like this happen so soon after he left. He might have found the stolen car himself and concluded that it was a good chance to pay off his grudge. Or he may have found the car hidden here and deliberately put the fishing rod in the seat so it would appear that you knew something about it. I wouldn't be at all surprised if Gus Montrose were mixed up in the affair in some way or another."

Jack's face flushed.

"I wish I had him here right now. I'd make him talk!"

"Just sit tight," advised Frank. "I know things look pretty bad, but something may turn up. We'll see if perhaps we can't do something for you."

Jack brightened up at this, for he knew that the help of the Hardy boys was not to be despised. The case looked black against him, but with Frank and Joe on his side he did not feel quite so disconsolate.

"Thanks, ever so much," he said gratefully. "I'm glad some one believes me."

"Those city detectives can't see any farther than the end of their noses," Chet Morton declared warmly. "Don't worry about them. If they put you in jail we'll dynamite the place to get you out." He grinned as he said this and his good humor alleviated the tension that had fallen over the group.

"Well, I guess we'll have to be going," said Frank, as he mounted his motorcycle. "Don't think too much about this, Jack. Something will turn up."

"I hope so," answered the boy.

Chet Morton and the Hardy lads said good-bye to their chum and rode out of the farmyard.

"No use chasing Mr. Fussy's car now," decided Joe.

"Gone but not forgotten," Chet said. "We might as well go home."

So, leaving Jack Dodd standing disconsolately in the yard, the three headed their motorcycles back toward Bayport.

CHAPTER IV

Out on Bail

On the following Monday, Frank and Joe Hardy noticed that Jack Dodd was not at school. They had heard no more about the case, although the disappearance of Isaac Fussy's automobile had increased public interest in the car thefts and the local newspapers were making much of the failure of the police to bring the thieves to justice.

The Bayport Automobile Club had already taken action by offering a reward of $500 for information leading to the recovery of any of the stolen cars and the arrest of those responsible. Three of the victims had also posted rewards of varying amounts, comprising another $500 all told, for the return of their automobiles. The affairs had mystified Bayport because of the fact that not a trace of any of the cars had been found, save in the case of Martin's Packard, and motorists were apprehensive. No one knew whose turn would come next.

As the Hardy boys were on their way to school on Tuesday morning Frank pointed out one of the Automobile Club posters in a window.

"I sure wish we could land those car thieves. That's a nice fat reward."

"If we caught the thieves we'd likely get the cars, too," replied Joe. "A thousand dollars is a nice little bit of money."

"It would come in handy. Added to the rewards we collected in the other cases, we'd have a good fat bank account."

"Reward or no reward, I'd like to catch the thieves just for the satisfaction of clearing up the affair. Most of all, so we could prove the Dodds haven't had anything to do with it."

"I wonder if the police have done anything about Jack yet. He surely was mighty blue on Saturday."

"Can't blame him," Joe said. "I'd be blue myself if I was accused of stealing a car I'd never even seen before."

As the Hardy boys entered the school they were met by Chet Morton, who called them over to one side.

"Have you heard?" he asked.

"About what?"

"About Jack Dodd and his father?"

"No. What's happened?"

"They were arrested last night for stealing Martin's car. They're both in the Bayport jail right now."

There was a low whistle of consternation from Frank.

"Isn't that a shame!" he declared indignantly. "They had no more to do with stealing that car than the man in the moon!"

"Of course, it was found on their farm," Chet pointed out. "I know they didn't do it, but you can't blame the police for taking action, when you come to think it over. The public are raising such an uproar about these missing cars that they have to do something to show they're awake."

"It's too bad Jack and his father should be made the goats."

"Sure is."

"They're in jail now?" asked Joe.

Chet nodded. "They're coming up for hearing this morning, but it's sure to be remanded. It's mighty tough, because they haven't much money and it will be hard for them to raise bail."

Chet's news disturbed the Hardy boys profoundly. For that matter, it had a depressing effect on all the boys in the class, for Jack Dodd was well liked and all his chums were quite convinced of his innocence of the charge against him. At recess they gathered in little groups, discussing the misfortune that had befallen him, and at noon a number of the lads stopped Officer Con Riley on the street and asked if he had heard the outcome of the morning's hearing.

"Remanded," said Riley briefly.

"For how long?"

"A week. They'll get about five years each, I guess. Been too much of this here car stealing goin' on."

"They're not convicted yet," Frank Hardy pointed out.

"They will be," declared Riley confidently. "We got the goods on 'em."

It was one of Mr. Riley's little eccentricities that he preferred to refer to the entire Bayport police force as "we," as though he had charge of most of its activities instead of being merely a patrolman on the beat adjacent to the high school.

"Got the goods on them—nothing!" snorted Chet Morton. "A car was found on the Dodd farm, that's all."

"It's enough," said the unruffled Con. "Men have been hung on less evidence than that."

"Are the Dodds out on bail?" Frank inquired.

The officer shook his head.

"Couldn't raise it," he said. "They've gotta stay in the coop."

"Even if they may be found innocent later on!" exclaimed Chet.

"That's the law," said Riley imperturbably. "If they can dig up five thousand dollars bail they'll be free until the case comes up."

"Five thousand! They'll never be able to raise that much money!"

"Then," said Officer Riley, as he stalked away, "they'll stay in the coop."

Frank and Joe Hardy went home thoughtfully. At lunch, their father noticed their preoccupation and asked what the matter was. They told him the whole story, of the discovery of the automobile on the farm, the finding of the rod, Jack's repeated declarations of innocence.

"I'm sure he didn't do it," Frank declared. "He's just not that sort of fellow. And his father is as honest as—as you are."

"Thanks for the compliment," laughed Fenton Hardy. "And you say they're being held on five thousand dollars bail."

Joe nodded. "They'll never raise it. I wonder, Dad, if we could—if you'd help us fix it up."

The boys looked at their father hopefully.

"Joe and I can put up some of our reward money," interjected Frank. "We hate to see the Dodds kept in jail."

Mr. Hardy was thoughtful.

"You must have great faith in them."

"We have," Frank declared. "They had nothing to do with stealing the car, we're certain. It seems tough that they should have to stay in jail just because it was found on their property."

"It's the law of the land. However, as you say, it is rather hard on them. If you lads have enough confidence in the Dodds to put up some of your own money for their bail, I suppose I can do the same. I'll make up the rest of the five thousand."

"Hurray!" shouted Joe. "I knew you'd say that, Dad!"

Mrs. Hardy smiled indulgently from the end of the table. Aunt Gertrude, a peppery old lady who was visiting the Hardys at the time, sniffed in derision. Aunt Gertrude was a maiden lady of advancing years who had very little faith in human nature.

"Chances are they'll go out and steal another car and run away," she snapped.

"Waste of money, I call it."

"I'll take my chances with the boys," laughed Mr. Hardy.

"Five thousand dollars gone!" Aunt Gertrude predicted.

"I don't think it'll be as bad as all that, Aunty," said Frank, winking at his brother.

"Wait and see, young man. Wait and see. I've lived in this world a good deal longer than you have—"

"Years longer," said Joe innocently.

This reference to her age drew a glare of wrath from over Aunt Gertrude's spectacles.

"I'm older than you are and I know the ways of the world. It seems you can't trust anybody nowadays."

However, in spite of Aunt Gertrude's doleful predictions, Fenton Hardy stood by his promise, and after lunch was over he went with the boys to the office of the District Attorney, where they put up bail to the amount of five thousand dollars for the release of Jack Dodd and his father, pending trial.

In a few minutes, father and son were free. When they learned the identity of their benefactors their gratitude was almost unbounded.

"We'd have been behind the bars right until the day of the trial," declared Mr. Dodd. "I don't know how to thank you. I give you my word you'll have no cause to regret it."

"We know that," Mr. Hardy assured him. "Don't worry."

"You're real chums!" declared Jack to the boys.

"Forget it," Joe said, embarrassed. "You'd do the same for us if it were the other way around."

"If you run across any information that might help us find who left the car on your farm let us know," put in Frank. "And, by the way, see if you can find out where Gus Montrose is now and what he is doing I have an idea that fellow knows something."

"I haven't heard anything about him, but I'll try to find out," Jack promised. "Are you going back home now?"

"I don't know. I hate to miss any more school, for I've been a bit behind in my work."

"Go on to school with the boys," advised Mr. Dodd. "I'll go back home alone. No use losing any more time than can be helped."

Fenton Hardy nodded his head in approval of this sensible advice and the boys went on to school together, where Jack Dodd received an enthusiastic welcome from his classmates, all of whom stoutly asserted their belief in his innocence and confidently predicted that he would come through his ordeal with flying colors.

"It's a crying shame ever to have arrested you," said one of the lads loyally.

"Oh, the police of this town are a lot of doughheads," said another.

"It's not the fault of the police, exactly," Frank pointed out. "It was also the state troopers and detectives."

"But Jack is innocent," came from several of the lads in unison.

"Of course he is—and so is his father," answered Joe.

16

"Gee, if only they round up the real thieves!" sighed one of the other boys. "Why, my dad won't let me park our car anywhere near the Shore Road any more!"

"My dad is getting so he won't hardly park anywhere," added another lad, and at this there was a general laugh.

"Those thieves are getting on everybody's nerves—they ought to be rounded up."

"Yes, and the sooner the better," declared Frank.

The kind words of his chums were very pleasing to Jack Dodd. Yet he was very sober as he entered the school building. He could not help but think of what might happen if he and his father could not clear their name.

"We may have to go to prison after all," he sighed dolefully.

CHAPTER V

More Thieving

After school the following afternoon, the Hardy boys repaired to the boathouse at the end of the street, where they kept their fast motorboat, the *Sleuth*.

They had bought this boat out of money they had received as a reward for their work in clearing up the mystery of the Tower Treasure and in the capture of a band of smugglers. It was a speedy craft, and the boys had enjoyed many happy hours in it.

Tony Prito, one of their chums, an Italian-American lad, also owned a motorboat, the *Napoli*, as did Biff Hooper, the proud skipper of the *Envoy*. Tony's boat had been the fastest craft on Barmet Bay until the arrival of the *Sleuth*, and there was much friendly rivalry between the boys as to the speed of their respective boats.

Chet Morton was sitting in the *Sleuth*, awaiting Joe and Frank by appointment.

"Come on," he said. "Tony and Biff are out in the bay already."

The Hardy boys sprang into their craft, and in a few minutes the *Sleuth* was nosing its way out into Barmet Bay. The boys could see the other boats circling about, as Tony and Biff awaited their arrival. Tony waved to them and in a short time they drew alongside the *Napoli*.

"Where shall we go?" shouted Frank.

"Anywhere suits me. Might as well just cruise around."

There was a roar as the *Envoy* surged up, with Biff at the wheel. Jerry Gilroy and Phil Cohen were with him.

"I don't suppose you want to go to Blacksnake Island, do you, Biff?" called out Joe.

"I'll say I don't! Once is enough."

"Me, too," chimed in Chet, as the three boats, running abreast, headed in the direction of Barmet village.

Blacksnake Island, out in the open sea some distance down the coast, had been the scene of perilous adventures for the chums. Some time previous Chet Morton and Biff Hooper had gone out in Biff's launch and had been kidnaped by a gang of crooks who mistook them for the Hardy boys and who wished to revenge themselves upon Fenton Hardy. They had been taken to Blacksnake Island, as has already been told in the fourth volume of this series, "The Missing Chums."

"I never want to see the place again," shouted Biff. "I had enough of it to last me a lifetime."

"Between snakes and crooks, we had plenty of excitement," Frank said.

"Excitement!" declared Chet, settling back comfortably. "Why, I am sure that was nothing."

"What do you mean, nothing?" demanded Joe. "If anything more exciting ever happened to you, I'd like to hear of it."

"Haven't I ever told you of the time I was the only survivor of a shipwreck that cost ninety-four lives?"

His comrades looked at Chet suspiciously. Chet Morton's joking proclivities were well known. His jests were invariably harmless, but he dearly loved a laugh and some of his hair-raising fictions were famous among the boys.

"First time I've ever heard of it," Frank said, "When were you ever in a shipwreck that cost ninety-four lives?"

"Off Cape Cod in '23," declared Chet dramatically. "It was the night the good ship *Brannigan* went down with all on board. Ah, but that was a terrible night. As long as I live, I'll never forget it! Never!"

"I don't think you even remember it," sniffed Frank.

But Chet went on, getting up steam.

"The *Brannigan* left Boston harbor at four bells and there was a dirty sea running, with a stiff breeze from the north. I had booked my passage early in the morning, but as sailing time approached, my friends beseeched me not to go. 'It is death!' they told me. But I merely laughed. 'Chet Morton is not afraid of storms. I shall sail.' The *Brannigan* was not out of sight of shore before the storm broke in all its fury. Thunder and lightning and a roaring rain! It was the worst storm in twenty years, the captain said. The passengers huddled in their cabins, sick with fear. Some of them were seasick too. The storm grew worse."

"This sounds like a big whopper," declared Joe, interested in spite of himself.

Chet's face was solemn as he continued.

"Night fell. The waves rolled over the staunch little ship. The helmsman clung to the wheel. Down in the lee scuppers—whatever they are—the first mate lay with a broken leg. Down in the forecastle the crew talked mutiny. Then came a dreadful cry. 'A leak! The ship has sprung a leak!' And, by golly, it had. The skipper came down from the bridge. 'Take to the boats,' he cried. 'Women and children first.' But the *Brannigan* was sinking fast by the stern. Before they could launch a single boat the ship sank swiftly, and eighty-five people went to a watery grave."

He shook his head sadly, as though reflecting on this horrible tragedy.

"Eighty-five?" said Frank. "A little while ago you told us ninety-four."

"Ninety-four lives," Chet pointed out. "Eighty-five people, but ninety-four lives. The ship's cat was drowned too."

Joe snorted as he saw how neatly Frank had fallen into the trap. Frank looked foolish. Then Joe spoke, chuckling.

"And you were the only survivor!" he exclaimed. "How did you escape?"

Chet stood up and gazed out over the waves.

"I missed the boat," he explained gently.

Joe glared wrathfully at the jester, then jumped for the wheel. He bore down on it so suddenly that the nose of the *Sleuth* veered into the wind, and Chet was thrown off his balance, sitting down heavily in the bottom of the craft, with a yelp of surprise. "That'll teach you!" said Joe grimly, struggling to suppress his laughter at Chet's melodramatic tale of the shipwreck. But the plump youth only grinned.

"Oh, boy, how you both bit!" he exploded. "How you gaped! You didn't know whether to believe it or not!" He roared with laughter. "Wait till I tell the others about this. 'How about the other nine lives?' 'How did *you* escape?' Wow!" He sat in the bottom of the boat and laughed until the tears came to his eyes. Frank and Joe joined in the laugh against themselves, for they were accustomed to Chet by now. Biff and Tony steered their boats over toward the *Sleuth* to learn the cause of all this mirth, but the boys refused to enlighten them as Chet wanted to reserve the yarn for a more convenient occasion when he might have some fresh victims.

For over an hour, the three motorboats raced about the bay, until the boys were aware that it was time to go home. The *Sleuth* reached the boathouse first, with the *Napoli* close behind, Biff Hooper's craft bringing up the rear. The launches safely in the slips, the six boys went up the street toward their homes.

"Going to try for the rewards?" asked Jerry Gilroy of the Hardy boys.

Frank smiled. "We won't turn them down if we happen to run into the auto thieves," he said. "A thousand dollars is a lot of money."

"Not to you," said Biff. "What do you two want with money after landing a fat reward in that gold case out West?"

He was referring to a case centering about some missing gold, in which the boys had gone all the way to Montana from their home on the Atlantic coast in order to help their father, who had fallen ill while tracking down the criminals.

Their good work in this case had netted them a handsome sum of money and they had the satisfaction of seeing their friend Jadbury Wilson, an old-time prospector who had come to Bayport to live, relieved from poverty. He had been one of the original owners of the gold and, following its disappearance, had fallen upon evil days.

"One can always use more money, you know," said Frank. "It'll come in handy if ever we go to college."

"I'll tell the world!" declared Chet. "Your father won't have to worry much about that. I wish my dad could say the same."

They had now reached the Hardy home and Frank and Joe said good-bye to their chums. When they went into the house they found that supper was almost ready. Aunt Gertrude sniffed, as they appeared, and expressed her amazement that they had managed to get home before mealtime. "For a wonder!" she said grimly.

Fenton Hardy emerged from his study. His face was serious.

"Well," he said, "I suppose you've heard the latest development?"

The boys looked at him blankly.

"Development in what?" asked Joe.

"In the car thefts."

"We haven't heard anything," Frank said. "Have they found the thieves?"

Mr. Hardy shook his head.

"No such luck. The thieves are still very much at large."

"You don't mean to say another car was stolen?" exclaimed Joe.

"Not only one. Two cars."

"Two more?"

Their father nodded.

"Two brand new autos, a Franklin and a Studebaker, were stolen last night," he told them. "Right in the city."

"Good night! And there's been no trace of them?"

"Not a sign. The police kept it quiet all day, hoping to recover them without any fuss, but they've had to admit themselves beaten. The cars have absolutely disappeared."

Aunt Gertrude spoke up.

"Mighty funny there were no cars stolen while those Dodds were in jail," she said pointedly. "The minute they get out—away go two new automobiles."

The boys glanced at one another uncomfortably. They were quite convinced that Jack Dodd and his father were innocent of any complicity in the car thefts, but they had to admit to themselves that their aunt had expressed a suspicion that might be commonly maintained throughout Bayport.

"The Dodds didn't have anything to do with it," said Fenton Hardy quietly. "I'm sure of that. Still—it looks bad."

"It certainly does!" declared Aunt Gertrude.

Frank turned to his brother.

"It's time for us to get busy," he said. "We'll go out on the Shore Road again to-morrow afternoon."

CHAPTER VI

On the Shore Road

The Hardy boys were not the only investigators on the Shore Road the next afternoon.

The daring thefts of the two new cars from the very streets of Bayport had aroused public resentment to a high pitch and the police were thrown into a flurry of activity. Motorists were beginning to clamor for action; no one dared leave his car parked on the street without seeing that it was securely locked, even if only for a few minutes; the Automobile Club held a meeting at noon and passed a resolution urging Chief Collig to put all his available men on the case.

The Shore Road was patrolled by Bayport police and detectives, as well as by state troopers. All outgoing automobiles were stopped and credentials demanded of the drivers. It was a case, however, of locking the stable door after the horse was stolen, for no more cars disappeared that day.

Most of the people who were stopped took the matter good-naturedly, but some were exceedingly bitter.

"How dare you take me for a thief?" shrilled Miss Agatha Mitts, a rich and peppery maiden lady who lived in an ancient mansion down the coast. "It's outrageous! I won't show my license!"

"You'll have to or go to jail," answered the trooper who had halted her.

"The idea! How dare you talk to me like that? You know well enough who I am!"

"Sorry, but I don't know you from Adam. And, anyway, it doesn't make any difference. Show your license or I'll take you to the lock-up."

"I am Miss Agatha Middleton Mitts, of Oldham Towers," said the maiden lady heatedly. "And I—"

"Going to show your license or not? If you haven't one—"

"Oh, yes, I've got a license. But I want you to understand—"

"Let me see it, quick. You are holding up traffic."

"Well, it's outrageous, anyway," sighed, Miss Mitts. But she had to rummage through her bag for the card and show it. Then she drove on, threatening all sorts of punishment to all the troopers in sight.

Drawn by the hope of earning the rewards offered for the apprehension of the thieves and recovery of the missing cars, a number of amateur detectives went scouting around the adjoining townships, harassing innocent farmers who had already been badgered and pestered into a state of exasperation by the officials. The Dodd family, in particular, suffered from these attentions. The Hardy boys and Chet Morton dropped in to see Jack Dodd and found him sitting disconsolately on top of the barnyard fence.

"It's bad enough to have detectives and troopers coming around and asking us to account for every minute of our time since we were let out on bail," said Jack; "but when nosey people come prying and prowling around, it's a little too much."

"You're not the only ones," consoled Frank. "Every farmer around Bayport has been chasing sleuths off the grounds all day."

"They keep popping up from behind the woodshed and under fences, like jack rabbits," said Jack, with a grin. "I suppose it would be funny if we hadn't gone through so much trouble already. One chap sat up in an apple tree half the morning watching the house. He thought we couldn't see him. I suppose he expects to catch us driving a stolen car into the barn."

"Is he there yet?" asked Chet.

Jack nodded.

"He went away for a while. I guess he went home for lunch, but he came back. He's patient. I'll say that much for him. He's up in the tree now, with a pair of field-glasses."

"The genuine detective!" said Chet approvingly. "Does he know you saw him?"

Jack shook his head.

"We didn't pay any attention. I suppose he thinks he's been very clever."

"Well, if he likes sitting in a tree so much, he'll have enough to suit him for a long while. You have a dog, haven't you, Jack?"

Jack nodded. "A bulldog. I'll call him." He whistled sharply, and in a few minutes an extremely ferocious looking bulldog came around the corner of the house, wagging his tail.

"Fine! Got a chain for him?"

The boys looked at Chet, puzzled, but Jack went away and returned with a long chain, which he attached to the dog's collar.

"I don't think you should let a dog run around loose," said Chet gravely. "It isn't good for him. I think he'd better be chained up. And if you'll show me just which apple tree contains our detective friend I'll show you the apple tree that should shelter Towser."

The others were beginning to see Chet's plan now. The Hardy boys grinned in anticipation.

"It's the tree right beside the orchard gate," said Jack. "You can see it from here."

"Come, Towser," said Chet, and stalked away. The bulldog waddled obediently behind, the chain clinking.

Chet went into the orchard and, without looking up, without giving any sign that he had noticed the man perched in the leafy branches above, he snapped the chain around the tree trunk, leaving Towser sitting in the shade. The bulldog looked puzzled, but he made no protest and settled down on his haunches.

"I guess that will hold our inquisitive friend for a while," said Chet cheerfully, as he came back with the air of one who had just accomplished a worthy deed. "If he wants to leave that tree, he'll have to argue the matter with Towser."

Hastily, the boys retired behind the stable so that the victim in the tree would not witness their mirth. They peeked around the corner every little while to see if there was any disturbance in the orchard, but the watcher stayed where he was, probably waiting for the dog to fall asleep.

"He'll get tired of that," predicted Chet, with a snicker. "I think we will see some action around that apple tree before long."

Just then the boys spied a familiar figure coming down the lane. A car was parked out in the main road and a bulky, stolid man was advancing toward them.

"Why, it's dear old Detective Smuff!" declared Chet.

Detective Smuff was one of the detectives on the Bayport police force. He was a worthy man, not over blessed with brains, and as a detective his successes had been mainly due to a dogged persistence rather than to any brilliant deductive abilities. Three of the cases on which he had been engaged had been solved by the Hardy boys, which had not tended to increase his liking for the lads, but he was cordial enough and bore no malice.

"Hello, Mr. Smuff," Frank called.

The detective nodded ponderously.

"More amatoors," he sighed. "What chance has a regular officer on a case like this when everybody else in town is puttin' their oar in?"

"Working on the car thefts?" asked Joe.

"I am." Smuff turned to Jack Dodd, "Just where were you, night before last, young man?"

"At home," replied Jack shortly. "There's no use asking me any more questions, Mr. Smuff. Chief Collig was out here yesterday morning and Dad and I were able to satisfy him that we hadn't been out of the house all evening."

"Oh," said Smuff, evidently disappointed. "The Chief was here, was he?"

"Yes."

"Well, I guess there ain't any use of me askin' questions, then," returned the detective.

"No sign of any of the cars, officer?" Frank asked.

"Not a trace."

"Any word from the other towns?"

Detective Smuff shook his head.

"There was three different ways they could have gone," he said. "The Shore Road branches off into three roads and we've sent men out along every one of 'em and every inch of the highway has been searched. Them cars have just plain vanished."

"The police in the other towns didn't see them?"

"No reports at all."

"Perhaps they were taken right through Bayport and out the other side," Joe suggested.

"They weren't taken through Bayport. Th& cars were missed within five minutes after they were stolen and all the patrolmen were told about 'em and kept a lookout. There was nobody on the Shore Road side, so this is the only way they could have come without bein' stopped. That's what makes it so queer," went on Detective Smuff. "The police in the other towns was given word and they were waitin' for the cars if they came through, but they never showed up."

"Then the cars must be hidden somewhere along the Shore Road!" Frank exclaimed.

"Looks like it. But we've searched every inch of the ground, and there's no place they *could* be hid." Detective Smuff shook his head sadly. "It's a deep case. A deep case. Well, I'll do my best on it," he said, with the air of a martyr.

"I'm sure you will," said Chet. He did not add that his private opinion of Detective Smuff's "best" was far from high.

A terrific barking from the direction of the orchard interrupted the conversation. The detective looked up, surprised. A loud howl and a protesting voice added to the uproar.

"The chap in the tree!" shouted Chet. He raced around the corner of the stable, and the others quickly followed. Detective Smuff, left alone, looked around in bewilderment, then jogged heavily after the boys.

Towser, beneath the apple tree, was doing his duty as guardian. The amateur detective in the tree had attempted to escape, perhaps lulled to a sense of false security because Towser had apparently gone into a doze. He was half way down the tree trunk now, and the bulldog was leaping and snapping at him from beneath. The chain was just long enough to hold the dog in check, and he fell short of the unfortunate victim by a few inches; but the frightened sleuth was unable to scramble back to safety and was clinging wretchedly to the tree, unable to retreat or descend. In the meantime he roared loudly for help.

Chet burst into peals of laughter, and the others, in spite of their sympathy for the inquisitive one in his plight, could restrain themselves no longer. The boys shrieked with merriment, Towser barked and leaped in renewed fury, and Detective Smuff came waddling up, audibly wondering what it was all about.

A whistle from Jack Dodd, as soon as he was able to stifle his laughter sufficiently, attracted Towser's attention. He stopped barking and looked inquiringly at his master.

"Down!" shouted Jack.

Obediently, the dog lay down.

"He won't hurt you."

The man in the tree, somewhat reassured, began to descend. The dog, beyond a low growl or two, paid no further attention. The moment the spy reached the ground he started for the fence at a run, scrambled over it and headed across the field toward the open road.

"What was he doing?" asked Detective Smuff suspiciously.

"Watching us," Jack returned. "Seems as if half the people in the county have their eye on us since those cars were stolen. I think that chap is cured."

"He should be," said Smuff, gazing respectfully at Towser. "If any one bothers you after this, let me know. Us regular detectives can't have any one buttin' into our work like that."

He glanced severely at the Hardy boys as he spoke.

"We certainly can't," said Joe innocently. Then, as Detective Smuff glared, he turned to his companions. "Come on, fellows. Let's take a look through the woods on the other side of the road. We might find some trace of the cars there."

CHAPTER VII

Gus Montrose

Detective Smuff walked back as far as the road with the boys, and then clambered into his car, where another detective on the Bayport force was waiting for him.

"You're just wastin' your time hunting through the woods," he told the boys heavily. "A car couldn't get down there, anyway, and we've hunted through there pretty thoroughly in the second place."

"It'll give us something to do," Frank said cheerfully.

"Keep you out of mischief, I guess," agreed Smuff, as though this were some consolation at any rate. He nodded to the boys and the car sped off toward Bayport.

"Dumb but good-hearted," said Chet.

"He isn't a bad sort," Joe remarked. "He's no great shakes as a detective, that's sure, but there are lots worse."

The boys crossed the road and struck off down a narrow trail that led through the undergrowth into the woods on the sloping land between the Shore Road and Barmet Bay. For the most part there were steep bluffs lining the bay, but at this point the declivity was more gradual.

"I think he's right about searching down through here," said Jack Dodd dubiously. "A car could never get down into this bush."

"A car mightn't but the car thieves might," Frank pointed out. "It seems mighty queer that none of the stolen cars have been traced at either end of the Shore Road. Those automobiles stolen the other night should have been picked up in one of the three towns on the branch roads. Smuff said the thefts were discovered in plenty of time to send out warning."

"It does seem strange. Out of so many cars, you'd imagine at least one or two would have been traced outside Bayport."

"I have a hunch that this whole mystery begins and ends right along the Shore Road," said Frank. "It won't hurt to scout around and see what we can find. Maybe there's a hidden machine shop where they alter the appearance of the autos."

"I was reading of a case in New York City not long ago," remarked Joe, as they pushed along. "The auto thieves got cars downtown and drove them to some place uptown. The police followed half a dozen gangsters for two weeks before they got on to their trick, which was to drive into an alleyway that looked as if it came to an end at the back of a barn. They found that a section of the side of the barn went up like a sliding door. The thieves would drive in with a stolen car. Inside the old barn was an elevator running down to a cellar. In the cellar was a machine and paint shop and five or six workmen down there could so alter a car in a few hours that the owner himself couldn't tell his own machine."

"Can you beat it!" exclaimed Chet. "Gee, it's a wonder they wouldn't work at something honest!"

Among the woods on the slope the boys wandered aimlessly. The sun cast great shafts of light through openings in the leaves above and once in a while they could catch glimpses of the blue waters of the bay in the distance.

Frank was in the lead. He was proceeding down a narrow defile in the forest when the others saw him suddenly stop and turn toward them with a finger on his lips, cautioning silence.

They remained stock-still until he beckoned to them, and then moved quietly forward, their feet making no noise in the heavy grass.

"I heard voices," Frank whispered as they came up to him.

"Ahead?" asked his brother.

Frank nodded.

"We'll go easy."

He moved on cautiously and the others followed. In a few moments they heard a dull murmur of voices and smelled the unmistakable odor of a wood fire. So far they could see no one, but soon the faint trail wound around in the direction of a clearing ahead and those in the rear saw Frank crouch among the bushes, peering through the leaves.

Quietly, the others came up. The four boys gazed through the undergrowth at the scene in the grassy clearing.

Three men were seated about a small fire, over which one was holding a tin pail suspended from a green branch. They were unshaven, frowsy-headed, untidy fellows, and they sprawled on the ground in careless attitudes.

"Tramps," whispered Chet, but Frank pressed a restraining hand on his arm. There was one thought in the minds of the four boys—that this trio might be the automobile thieves!

"Not far from Bayport, are we?" growled one of the men.

"Not many miles farther on," replied the man holding the branch.

"It's the first time I've ever been in these parts."

"It ain't so bad," volunteered the third man, lighting his pipe. "Easy pickin's around the farmhouses. It didn't take me ten minutes to rustle that grub to-night."

"You did well, Bill," said the man at the fire, glancing at a package of food near by. "I wonder where that guy is that we met on our way in here? He gave us a funny look."

"He minded his own business, anyway."

"Good thing for him that he did. I don't hold with bein' asked questions."

"Me neither. A good rap over the dome for anybody that wants to know too much—that's my motto."

"Is that mulligan ready?"

"Not yet. We'll be eatin' in about five minutes."

Frank turned and gestured to the others, indicating that they might as well withdraw. It seemed clear to him that these men were simply tramps preparing their evening meal in the shelter of the woods, and nothing would be gained by making their presence known.

Jack Dodd and Joe turned and moved silently away, but the luckless Chet had not gone two paces before he tripped over a root and fell sprawling on the ground, with a grunt of pain and surprise.

One of the tramps looked up.

"What was that?"

"Somebody in the bushes," said another.

The two men scrambled to their feet and came directly toward the boys. Jack and Joe took to their heels, but Frank waited to help Chet up and the delay was fatal. The tramps came crashing through the bushes and caught sight of them.

"Kids, eh?" roared one. He sprang toward Frank and caught him by the shoulder. The other seized Chet. Joe and Jack were out of sight beyond the trees by now and the tramps were evidently unaware of their presence.

"Take your hands off me," said Frank coolly.

Somewhat taken aback, the tramp regarded him for a moment in a surly manner. "What do you mean by spying on us?" he demanded.

"We weren't spying on you."

"What brings you around here, then?"

The other tramp had abandoned the pail of stew at the fire and came through the bushes toward them.

"What's the matter?" he asked. "What's goin' on here?"

"A couple of kids spyin' on us," said Frank's captor, and tightening his grip on the boy's shoulder.

"We oughta skin 'em alive," declared the newcomer. "How long have you been hiding in them bushes, boy?"

"We just came up a minute ago and when we heard voices we looked to see who was there. We were just going away."

"You were, eh? What were you going away for?"

"It wasn't any of our business if you wanted to cook your supper in the woods."

This answer seemed to placate the tramps, for they glanced from one to the other, seemingly reassured.

"You weren't going for the police?" asked one suspiciously.

Both boys shook their heads.

"Did somebody send you here?"

"No. We were just wandering through the wood and we came on your fire."

"That fellow we met a little while ago didn't send you here, did he?"

"We haven't seen anybody," said Frank. "What did he look like?"

"Thin, hard-lookin' guy with a hook nose."

"We haven't seen any one like that."

"He was prowling around here a little while ago," said the tramp, in a more friendly tone. "I guess you boys are all right. If we let you go will you promise not to run and tell the police?"

"Oh, sure!" piped Chet, in vast relief.

"We're not doin' any harm here. We're just three poor chaps that's out of work and we're on our way to Bayport to look for a job," whined one of the others. "You wouldn't set the police on us, would you?"

"It's none of our business who you are or what you're doing," Frank assured them. "We won't mention seeing you."

"All right, then." His captor released his grip on Frank's shoulder. "Beat it away from here and don't bother us again."

The two boys lost no time in making their way out of that vicinity. The three tramps stood watching until they disappeared beyond the trees at the bend in the trail, then went back to their fire.

Some distance away, Frank and Chet came upon the other boys, who had halted and were devising ways and means of rescue.

"Golly!" said Joe, "we thought you were in for it. We were just going to toss up and see who would go back to find out what had happened to you."

"Why couldn't you both come back?" Chet asked.

"We thought if one of us went back he might be caught too, and that would still leave somebody to go for help."

"Good idea. They were only tramps. Gave us a bit of a scare," said Chet airily. He had been almost frightened out of his wits. "We just talked right up to them and they let us go."

"I wonder who is this hook-nosed man they were talking about," said Frank. "They seemed to be worrying more about him than about us."

"A hook-nosed man?" exclaimed Jack Dodd. "What about him?"

"You remember when they were talking by the fire, they mentioned meeting somebody on their way into the wood. They asked us about him, and seemed to think he may have sent us in to spy on them."

"Thin, hard-looking chap," Chet remarked, remembering the description the tramp had given.

"Why, that must be—but it couldn't be *him*!" exclaimed Jack.

"Who?"

"Gus Montrose. The hired man that Dad discharged a little while ago. I was telling you about him. The description fits him exactly."

"I thought he went away," said Joe.

"We haven't seen him since he left the farm, but I've always had an idea he was prowling around."

Just then Frank clutched Chet's arm.

"Listen!"

The boys halted. They could plainly hear the sound of snapping twigs and a scuffing that indicated the approach of some one on the trail ahead. A moment later, a man came into view.

He stepped out from among the trees and came to a stop, staring at the lads, plainly astonished at seeing them. Then he wheeled about and sprang into the bushes. They could hear him plunging through the undergrowth as he disappeared.

Although they had only a momentary glance, the boys readily identified him as the man the tramps had mentioned. Disreputably clad, he was a thin man with a cruel mouth and a hooked nose.

"Gus Montrose!" exclaimed Jack Dodd.

CHAPTER VIII

The Missing Truck

"Let's tackle that fellow!" exclaimed Frank Hardy. "We can ask him about your fishing rod, Jack."

Frank scrambled into the bushes, where Gus Montrose had disappeared, and in a moment his companions were hurrying after him. But although Frank had lost little time making up his mind to question the former hired man, Montrose had been too quick for him. The fellow was nowhere to be seen.

"Shall I call to him?" asked Jack Dodd.

"You can if you want to," answered Frank. "I doubt if he'll answer."

"Might scare him into running faster," suggested Joe.

"I reckon he's running about as fast as he can now."

"Gus! Gus Montrose!" yelled Jack. "Come back here! We want to talk to you!"

All listened, but no reply came to this call.

"Silence fills the air profound," came soberly from Joe.

"So much noise it would wake a tombstone," added Chet.

Again Jack called, and with no better results.

"Let's all yell together," suggested Joe.

This was done, but no answer came back.

"Sorry, but I've got a date elsewhere," mimicked Joe. "Be back next month at three o'clock."

"That fellow is no good, and I know it," murmured Frank. "An honest man would come back and face us."

"Listen!" cried Jack, putting up his hand.

All listened with strained ears.

"Don't hear a thing—" began Chet.

"I hear it," interrupted Frank.

A snapping and crackling sound among the bushes ahead lured the boys on and they went plunging through the woods. They failed to catch sight of the quarry, however. Evidently Montrose was well acquainted with this part of the country, for after a while the sounds of his retreat died away.

Frank, who was in the lead, came to a stop, realizing that further pursuit was useless. In a few minutes the others came up, panting.

"Did he get away?" asked Joe.

Frank nodded. "He was too quick for us. When he knew we were after him he didn't lose any time."

"I wish we had been able to talk to the rascal," said Jack Dodd. "I would have had a few things to tell him."

"Probably we wouldn't have got much satisfaction out of him, anyway," Frank remarked. "Still, you could have asked him what he knew about that fishing rod."

"It's something to know that he's still hanging around this part of the country," pointed out Chet. "He has evidently been lying low since he left your farm."

"He's up to some mischief, I'm sure of that."

"Probably built himself a shack somewhere in the woods," suggested Joe.

"Well, we may run across him some other time. It's getting late and I think we'd better be starting home," said Frank.

Chet and Joe agreed that it was about time, and as there seemed little to be gained by continuing the search for Gus Montrose or for any evidence of the stolen cars, the boys retraced their steps back through the woods until they reached the Shore Road. Their motorcycles had been parked in the shelter of the trees.

"About time for my supper, too," said Jack Dodd. "If you're out this way again, look me up and we'll make another search through the woods."

His friends promised to do this and, bidding Jack good-bye, they mounted their motorcycles and were soon roaring off in the direction of Bayport. They had spent more time in the wood than they had been aware of, and were anxious to get back to the city without being too late for the evening meal. Mrs. Hardy seldom scolded, but the boys had vivid recollections of Aunt Gertrude's acid remarks on similar occasions.

They emerged on an open stretch of road where a sand embankment sloped steeply down to Barmet Bay. The beach lay beneath them at the foot of the sheer declivity and the waters of the bay sparkled in the rays of the late afternoon sun.

A movement on the beach caught Frank's eye and he brought his motorcycle to a sudden stop.

"What's the matter?" asked Joe, swerving wildly to avoid piling headlong into Frank's machine.

"Run out of gas?" inquired Chet, putting on the brakes.

But Frank had dismounted and was walking over to the side of the road, out on to the top of the embankment.

"There's somebody down on the beach."

"What of it? Somebody swimming or fishing. Do you mean to say you stopped just because of that?"

But Frank was gazing down the steep, sandy slope.

"There's something queer about this," he said slowly. "There are two men down there, lying on the sand."

Joe and Chet, immediately interested, came running over. The three boys looked down at the two figures on the beach far below.

"They're not asleep," said Joe. "One of them seems to be rolling around."

"They're tied!" shouted Frank. "Look! You can see the ropes! I was wondering what was so queer about them. Those men are tied hand and foot!"

Joe was examining the embankment at their feet.

"Why, they've been rolled down the side!" he exclaimed. "Look where the sand has been disturbed!"

True enough, sand and gravel at the top of the slope showed a distinct depression, and all the way down the embankment this depression continued, as though a heavy object had slid to the bottom.

From the beach below came a faint shout.

"Help! Help!"

The men on the shore had seen them.

"We'd better go down," said Frank. "I wonder if there isn't a path of some kind around here."

"Let's slide!" Chet suggested.

"We're liable to break our necks tobogganing down this slope. No, there should be a path."

Frank ran along the top of the embankment toward a clump of trees a few yards away, where the slope was not so steep, and there he found a foot-path that led a winding course down the side of the hill toward the beach. It wound about across the face of the slope and covered twice the distance they would have had to go if they had adopted Chet's suggestion, though it was a great deal surer. They emerged on the open shore eventually and saw the two bound figures lying on the beach not fifty yards off.

In a short time the boys were bending over the prostrate victims. The men, who were clad in overalls, were bound hand and foot with heavy rope, at which the lads slashed vigorously with their pocketknives.

The strands fell apart and the two men were able to sit up, rubbing their limbs, which had been chafed by the ropes in their efforts to free themselves.

"I thought we'd be here all night!" declared one of the men, a plump, grimy young fellow about twenty years of age.

"Mighty lucky thing for us that you saw us," said the other, who was older in appearance. "We shouted and shouted. At least a dozen cars must have passed along the road and no one saw us."

They got to their feet.

"What happened?" asked Frank. "How on earth do you come to be down here, tied up like this?"

"Hold-up!" said the older man briefly. He looked up toward the road, an anxious expression on his face. "I don't suppose you met a truck along the road anywhere?"

The boys shook their heads.

"It's gone, then," said the younger man with a gesture of resignation. "Six thousand dollars' worth of goods!"

"We'll have to get back to town and report this."

"We can take you back," said Frank quickly. "We have motorcycles up on the road."

"Fine. Let's hurry!"

The two men started back toward the path at a rapid gait and the three boys hurried along. As they ascended the slope, the plump young chap explained what had happened.

"We're truck drivers for the Eastern Importing Company, and we were bringing a load of silk into Bayport," he said. "Right at the top of the embankment we were held up by those two men."

"How long ago?" Joe asked.

"A little over an hour ago. They stepped out of the bushes, each man masked and carrying a revolver. Bill was at the wheel and I was on the seat beside him. They made him stop the truck and then they made us get down into the road. When we did that, one of the hold-up men covered us with his revolver while the other tied us up. He made a good job of it, too, I'll tell the world. We couldn't move hand or foot."

"How did they get you down onto the beach?"

"They rolled us down the embankment! Don't we look it?"

The clothes of both men had been badly tattered and torn, while their arms and faces also gave evidence of the bruises and lacerations they had suffered in their descent.

"I thought we'd roll clean into the bay," said the other man. "If we had, it would have been all up with us."

"We'd have been drowned, without a chance to save ourselves," his companion agreed. "As it was, we came pretty close to the water's edge, banged and battered from that toboggan slide, and then we just had to lie there until somebody came along and set us free. At first we thought some one would surely see us from the road, but as car after car went by we began to lose hope.

"I was afraid it would get dark and then no one would be able to see us, even if they did chance to look down this way. It wouldn't have been very pleasant, staying out on that beach all night."

"Did you see where the truck went to?" asked Frank.

The men shook their heads.

"The hold-up men drove away in it—that's all we know," said one.

"It took us a few minutes to recover our senses after the slide down the embankment, and by that time the truck was gone. Whether it went on toward Bayport, or turned around, we can't tell," added the other.

"It certainly didn't pass in the other direction," said Chet.

But Frank was dubious.

"We were down in the woods quite a while, remember," he pointed out. "It might have gone by during that time."

They regained the road.

"Perhaps we can find the marks of the tires," suggested Joe.

Assisted by the two men, the lads searched about in the dust of the roadway, but so many cars had passed in the intervening time that all trace of the truck had been obliterated.

"No use searching now," said the driver. "If you lads will get us into Bayport we'll report the case to the police."

They abandoned the quest and in a short time the party had arrived in the city, Frank and Joe taking the two men as passengers on their motorcycles. At the police station, the hold-up was duly reported and immediately word was flashed to the police in other cities and to officers out in the country.

But to no avail.

By nine o'clock that night there had been no report on the missing truck. It had not passed through any of the three cities at the other end of the Shore Road, and Bayport police were positive it had never entered the city. The truck, with its six thousand dollar cargo, had utterly disappeared.

CHAPTER IX

Following Clues

This new sensation soon had Bayport by the ears.

Although the owners of private cars had been content to leave the matter of their stolen property in the hands of the police, the Eastern Importing Company went a step farther. They not only demanded the fullest official investigation, but they retained Fenton Hardy to take up the case, as well. They were by no means resigned to losing a valuable load of silk without a struggle.

In his study, next day, Mr. Hardy called in his sons and told them the importing company had asked him to do what he could toward recovering the stolen goods. "Aside from my fee," he said, "they are offering a reward of five hundred dollars if the silk is returned to them. What I want to ask you is this—do you think there is any chance that the truck driver and his assistant may have been lying?"

The boys scouted this theory.

"I don't think so, Dad," returned Frank. "They told a perfectly straight story. As a matter of fact, they were so anxious to get to Bayport and report the robbery that it was some time before we could get them to tell us what actually happened."

"And they could never have tied themselves up as thoroughly as they were tied," Joe declared.

"Men have been known to rob their employers before this," said Mr. Hardy. "We can't afford to overlook any possibilities."

"I think you can afford to overlook that one, sir. These men were honest, I'm sure of that."

"Well, Frank, I'll trust your judgment. I've investigated the records of the two men and they have never had anything against them, so I suppose it was an honest-to-goodness hold-up."

"It was real enough. We could see the marks in the embankment where they had been rolled down from the road," put in Joe.

"I'm sorry they couldn't give a better description of the hold-up men. All they could say was that they were both of medium height and that they wore masks. It isn't very much to go on. However, I may be able to get a line on the case when they try to get rid of the silk. The stuff is bound to turn up sooner or later and I may be able to trace it back to the thieves."

However, although Fenton Hardy devoted the next two days to the case, he made little progress toward locating either the missing truck or its cargo. As in the case of the other stolen cars, the truck seemed to have vanished into thin air, and although its description was broadcast all through the state, and police officials and garage mechanics were asked to be on the lookout for it, the mystery remained unsolved.

One evening toward the latter part of the week, the Hardy boys mounted their motorcycles and rode down High Street in the direction of the Shore Road. This was in accordance with a plan made earlier in the day.

"It stands to reason that if any of the cars ever got out into the state, at least one or two of them would be found," said Frank. "I have a mighty strong hunch that the whole mystery begins and ends right along that road."

"Perhaps those tramps we saw in the woods might have something to do with it."

"They may have had something to do with the hold-up, although it's not very probable. They looked as if they'd been sitting around that fire for quite a while, and it was a good distance from the place where the truck was robbed. However, it won't hurt us to do a little sentry duty and keep an eye on the Shore Road. We may have our trouble for nothing, but you never know what will turn up."

The lads drove out the road to a point midway between the scene of the truck hold-up and the Dodd farm. It was growing dark by the time they drew their motorcycles beneath the shelter of some trees.

"We might as well wait right here," said Frank, making himself comfortable on the grass. "If we see anything suspicious we can follow it up."

In the heavy shade, the boys could not be seen from the road. They talked in whispers. They had no clear idea of what they expected to find, but they were convinced that the Shore Road hid the mystery of the stolen automobiles, and their experience in previous cases had taught them that patience was often rewarded.

A few cars passed by, some bound toward Bayport, others in the opposite direction, but they were obviously pleasure cars and there was nothing about them to arouse suspicion. Once in a while, through the trees on top of the bluff, the boys could see the twinkling lights of a boat out on Barmet Bay. In the summer night, the silence was only broken by the trilling of frogs in the ditches along the road.

Presently they heard voices.

There was no one approaching along the highway, but as the voices grew louder they appeared to come from a field beyond the fence. At that moment the moon appeared from behind a cloud, and in its ghostly light, the Hardy boys distinguished two figures moving toward them in the meadow.

Silently, the lads crouched in the shadow of the trees, watching.

"This is a good night for it," growled one of the men.

"It's a good night if we don't get caught."

Joe's hand tightened about Frank's arm.

"What are you worrying about? We won't get caught. It isn't the first time we've got away with it."

"Yes, I know. But, somehow, I'm nervous to-night. I'm afraid we'll land up in the police court some of these fine days."

"If you're scared, go on home. I'll go on alone," said the first man scornfully.

"I'm not scared! Who says I'm scared?"

"Well, if you're not scared, shut up. I know we're breakin' the law, but we've never been caught yet."

The men scrambled over the fence. The boys saw that the first fellow was carrying two long poles and that the other carried a bag over his shoulder.

"Have you got all the stuff?"

"Yes."

"We'd better not walk along the road. Somebody's liable to spot us. Keep to the shadow and then we'll cut down into the woods."

The men hastily crossed the road in the moonlight. They were only a few yards away from the boys but, fortunately, did not see them. In the dim light, the watchers could not distinguish the features of the pair.

"There's a path here somewhere, isn't there?" asked one.

"Don't you remember it? If it hadn't been for that path the other night we'd have been nabbed."

"That's right. You know this country pretty well."

"I should. I've lived around here long enough."

About fifty yards away, the men turned down toward the woods and vanished in the darkness of the trees. Their voices receded. Frank and Joe scrambled to their feet.

"Come on," said Frank, in excitement. "We'll follow them."

"Do you think they're the thieves?"

"I'm sure of it. They're up to some kind of monkey-business, anyway. We'll find out where they're going."

In the soft grass the boys made not a sound as they sped along in the shade of the trees toward the path the two men had taken. They found it without difficulty, a fairly well defined trail that was quite visible in the moonlight. The lads plunged into the depths of the woods and there the moonlight did not penetrate. They had to feel their way forward, moving slowly in order to keep their progress silent.

After a while they could hear the voices of the two men again, not far ahead.

"Go easy," one was saying. "You never know who's likely to be prowling around here these nights."

"Too many police been nosing around these parts to suit me."

"We've got to take those chances."

The boys emerged into a clearing on the slope just in time to see the two men disappearing into the heavy wood on the opposite side. The clearing lay wide and deserted in the bright moonlight.

"They're up to some mischief," said Frank. "We'll have to be careful they don't see us."

"I wonder what those long poles are for!"

"They're not fishing poles. Too short and straight for that."

"Well, we'll soon find out. I think we're on the trail of something big."

"I'm sure of it."

The boys sped across the clearing and went on down the trail through the dark wood beyond. They were drawing closer to a brook now and they could plainly hear the lapping of the water against the rocks in the distance. In this vicinity there were several brooks flowing down into Barmet Bay.

Frank suddenly came to a stop.

"Look!" he said.

The boys peered through the gloom.

Beyond the branches of the trees they saw a glimmer of light. It disappeared, then shone again, steadily.

CHAPTER X

The Great Discovery

"I'll bet that light's a signal light," whispered Joe Hardy to his brother.

The boys watched the yellow gleam among the trees. Then, slowly, the light began to move. It swung to and fro, as though it was being carried by some one, and finally vanished.

Frank led the way down the path. In a few minutes they heard a snapping of twigs that indicated that the two men were not far ahead. The path dipped sharply, down a rocky slope, sparsely covered with underbrush. Then the brook came into view. They could see the pair clearly now. One of the men was carrying a lantern; the other bore the long poles and the bag. Drawn up on the side of the brook, below the rocks and just above its mouth, the boys distinguished a small boat.

They crouched in the shelter of the bushes, and watched as the man who carried the lantern put the light down and strode over to a clump of trees from which he presently emerged, carrying a pair of oars. He dumped them into the boat with a clatter, which aroused the wrath of his companion.

"What do you think you're doing?" he demanded fiercely. "Want to rouse up everybody from here to Bayport?"

"I forgot," the other answered apologetically.

"Don't forget again."

"There's nobody around, anyway."

"Don't be too sure."

He fitted the oars in the rowlocks quietly, and the pair pushed the boat out into the brook.

"What shall we do?" whispered Joe. "Tackle them?"

"Wait a minute."

Hardly were the words out of Frank's mouth before he heard a rustling in the bushes almost immediately behind him. He looked around, startled, and saw a shadowy figure flit among the bushes, then another and another. He was so astonished that he almost cried out. Where had these newcomers appeared from? Who were they?

The Hardy boys pressed close to the ground as the three figures passed so close by them that they could almost have reached out and touched them. Not a word was said. The three men made their way silently past, in the direction of the brook.

"All right," said one of the men at the boat. "I guess we can start out now."

At that instant, the three newcomers sprang out from the depth of the brush. There was a wild yell from the man bent over the boat.

"Come on, boys!" shouted one of the attackers. "We got 'em!"

Trembling with excitement, the Hardy boys looked on. They saw the three men close in. One of the fellows at the boat made a dash for liberty but he was tripped up and flung heavily into the brook. The other fought back, but he was quickly overpowered. The struggle was sharp but brief, and in a few minutes the two men were prisoners and were taken out into the moonlight.

"You came once too often, Jed," said one of their captors. "We've been watchin' for you."

"You ain't got anythin' on us," said Jed.

"Oh, yes we have! Caught you red-handed. Any of your pals around?"

"Just the two of us."

"Boat, lantern and everything, eh? You were too sharp for us most of the time, Jed, but we were bound to catch you sooner or later."

Greatly puzzled by this dialogue, wondering who the newcomers were and wondering why Jed and his companion had thus been captured, the Hardy boys rose slightly from their hiding place to get a better view of proceedings.

Just then they heard a heavy footstep in the bushes immediately behind them. They dropped again to the earth, but it was too late. They had been seen.

"Who's there?" growled a husky voice, and some one came plunging in through the bushes toward them.

Frank got to his feet and scrambled wildly for safety. Joe did likewise. The man behind them gave a loud shout.

"Here's some more of 'em!" he called.

Joe tripped over a root and went sprawling. In the darkness it was almost impossible to see a clear way to safety. Frank paused to help his brother to his feet, and their pursuer was upon them. He seized Frank by the coat collar.

One of the other men came crashing through the underbrush.

"I've caught 'em!" announced their captor. "Two more."

The newcomer emerged from a thicket and pounced on Joe.

"Good work!" he said exultantly.

The Hardy boys were hauled roughly out of the bushes and down into the moonlight, where the two captives were being held.

"Caught 'em hiding right in the bushes," said the man who had discovered them, tightening his grip on Frank's collar.

"Boys, eh?" said the leader, coming forward and peering closely at them. "Since when have you had boys helping you, Jed?"

The prisoner called Jed looked at the Hardy boys suspiciously.

"I never saw 'em in my life before," he growled.

"What are they doing here, then?"

"How should I know?" asked Jed. "I tell you I don't know anything about them."

"Why were you hiding in those bushes?" demanded the leader, of Frank.

"We were watching those two men," Frank returned promptly, indicating Jed and his companion.

"Watching them? Helping them, you mean."

"We don't know yet what they were up to. We were watching the Shore Road for automobile thieves and we saw those men going down into the woods, so we followed them."

The boys were still completely mystified. Just what errand had brought Jed and the other man to this lonely place at that hour of night, and just who were their captors, remained a puzzle to them.

"You didn't come here to spear fish?"

"Spear fish?" exclaimed Frank.

"Don't be so innocent. You know Jed and this fellow were coming down to spear fish by night-light, and it's against the law!"

The whole situation was now clear. Frank and Joe felt supremely foolish. Instead of trailing two automobile thieves, they had merely been following two farmers of the neighborhood who had been engaged in the lawless activity of spearing fish by night. This explained the mysterious conversation and their allusions to fearing capture. The other men were nothing more or less than game wardens.

"We didn't know," said Frank. "We thought perhaps they were the auto thieves."

The game wardens began to laugh.

"You were on the wrong track that time, son," said one. "I guess they're all right, Dan. Let them go."

The man who had stumbled on them in the bush released Frank reluctantly.

"They gave me a start," he said. "Hidin' there so quiet. I was sure they were with this other pair."

"Never saw either one of them before," repeated Jed.

"Well, if you stand up for them, I guess they're telling the truth. You boys beat it out of here and don't go interfering with our work again. You might have scared these two away if they'd caught sight of you."

"I wish we had seen 'em," said Jed. "We wouldn't be in this mess now."

"You'd have been caught sooner or later. You've been spearing fish in the brooks and ponds around here for the past three weeks, and you know it. You'll stand a fine in police court to-morrow."

The Hardy boys did not wait to hear the rest of the argument. Sheepishly, they left the group, thankful to be at liberty again, and retraced their steps up the trail through the wood until they again reached the road. Neither said a word. This inglorious end to the adventure had left them crestfallen.

They mounted their motorcycles and drove back to Bayport. The house was in darkness. Quietly, they went up the back stairs and gained their bedroom.

"Spearing fish!" said Frank in a disgusted voice, as he began to unlace his boots. He glanced at Joe, who was grinning broadly, Then, as they thought of their cautious pursuit of the two fishermen and of their certainty that they had found the automobile thieves at last, they began to laugh.

"The joke is on us," snickered Joe.

"It sure is. I hope the game wardens don't tell any one about this."

"If Chet Morton ever gets hold of it we'll never hear the end of the affair."

But Chet, who had a way of picking up information in the most unexpected quarters, did hear of it.

CHAPTER XI

Fish

One of the game wardens chanced to live near the Morton farm, and as he was on his way into Bayport next morning to give evidence against the two men arrested, he fell in with Chet and in the course of their conversation chanced to mention the two boys who had so neatly blundered into the trap the previous night.

"Said they were lookin' for auto thieves," he chuckled.

"What did they look like?" asked Chet, interested.

"One was dark and tall. The other was about a year younger. A fair-haired chap."

Chet snorted. The Hardy boys! No one else.

"What are you laughin' about?" asked the game warden.

"Nothing. I just happened to think of something."

On his way to school, Chet stopped off at a butcher's shop long enough to purchase a small fish, which he carefully wrapped in paper. He was one of the first students in the classroom and he watched his opportunity, putting the parcel in Frank Hardy's desk. Then, before the Hardy boys arrived, he put in the time acquainting his chums with the events of the previous night, so that by the time Frank and Joe came in sight there was scarcely a student in the school who did not know of their blunder.

"It sure is one on the Hardy boys," remarked Tony Prito.

"I'll say it is," returned Biff Hooper. "They don't usually trip up like that."

"Trip up? They never do—that is, hardly ever," put in another pupil.

"They are the cleverest fellows in this burg," came from one of the other students.

"Of course, everybody falls down once in a while."

"Just the same, it must gall them to think of how they were fooled."

"You bet."

Frank and Joe did not at first notice the air of mystery and the grinning faces, as they entered the school yard, but they were soon enlightened. A freshman, apparently very much frightened, came over to them at Chet's bidding.

"Please," he said, "my mother wants to know if you'll call at our house after school."

"What for?" asked Joe.

"She wants to know if you have any fish to sell."

Whereupon the freshman took to his heels. There was a roar of laughter from a group of boys who were within hearing. The Hardy boys flushed. Then Chet approached.

"Hello, boys," he said innocently. "You look sleepy."

"Do we?"

"What's the matter? Been up all night?"

"No. We got lots of sleep."

"Fine. Little boys shouldn't stay out late at night. It's bad for 'em. By the way," continued Chet airily, "I'm going out fishing to-night. I wonder if you'd like to come and sit on the shore and watch me."

Frank took careful aim with an algebra and hurled it at the jester, but Chet dodged and took to flight, chuckling heartily.

"Fish!" shrieked Jerry Gilroy, from a point of vantage on the steps.

"Fresh fish!" roared Phil Cohen.

"Whales for sale—ten cents a pound," chimed in Biff Hooper.

"How on earth did they hear about it?" gasped Joe. "We're in for it now."

"Just have to grin and bear it. Let's get into the classroom."

Pursued by cries of "Fish!" the Hardy boys hastened into the schoolroom and sat down at their desks, where they took refuge in study, although the bell had not yet rung.

Chet came in.

"Not in police court this morning?" he asked politely. "I heard you had been arrested for spearing fish last night."

"Just you wait," retorted Frank darkly.

He thrust his hand into his desk for a book and encountered the package. In another moment he would have withdrawn it, but a suspicion of the truth dawned on him. He knew that Chet was a practical joker and, with a chance like this, almost anything might be expected. So, thinking quickly, he left the package where it was and took out a history. By the expression of disappointment on Chet's face he knew his suspicions had been correct.

There were still a few minutes before school opened.

"Get him out of the room," whispered Frank to his brother, as Chet went over to his own desk.

Mystified, Joe obeyed.

"Well," he said to their chum, "we can stand a bit of kidding. Come on out and I'll tell you all about it."

They went out into the hall. Frank took the package from his desk. The odor was enough. If ever a fish smelled fishy, it was that fish. One stride, and he was over at Chet's desk. In a moment the package was nestling among Chet's books and Frank was back at his own desk, working busily.

The bell rang.

The students came into the classroom, Chet among them. He sat down, chuckling at some private jest, and began opening his school bag. Mr. Dowd, the mathematics teacher, entered for the first class of the day. Mr. Dowd was a tall, lean man with very little sense of humor, and Chet Morton was one of his pet aversions.

He went up to his desk and looked around, peering through his glasses.

"First exercise," he announced. Most of the students had their textbooks in readiness, but Chet usually took his time. Mr. Dowd frowned. "Morton, where is your book?"

"Right here, sir," replied Chet cheerfully. He groped in the desk and took out the textbook. With a sickening thud, the package dropped to the floor.

Chet's eyes bulged. He recognized it in an instant. A guilty flush spread over his face.

"What have you there, Morton?"

"N-n-nothing, sir."

"Don't leave it lying there on the floor. Pick it up."

Chet gingerly picked up the package.

"Your lunch?" suggested Mr. Dowd.

"N-no, sir. I mean, yes, sir."

"Just what *do* you mean? Why are you looking at it with that idiotic expression on your face?"

"I—I didn't expect to find it there, sir."

"Morton, is this another of your jokes? If so, I wish you'd let us all enjoy it. Do you mind telling us what's in that package?"

"I—I'd rather not, sir. It's just a—a little present."

"A little present!" Mr. Dowd was convinced, by Chet's guilty expression, that there was more behind this than appeared on the surface. "Open it this instant."

"Please, sir—"

"Morton!"

Miserably, Chet obeyed. Before the eyes of his grinning schoolmates, he untied the string, removed the paper, and produced the fish. There was a gasp of amazement from Mr. Dowd and a smothered chuckle from every one else.

"A fish!" exclaimed the master.

"Y-yes, sir."

"What do you mean, Morton, by having a fish in your desk?"

"I—I don't know, sir."

"You don't know? Don't you know where the fish came from?"

Chet Morton, for all his jokes, always told the truth. He did know where the fish came from.

"Yes, sir," he answered feebly.

"Where?"

"Hogan's butcher shop."

"Did you buy it?"

"Yes, sir."

"And you brought it to school with you?"

"Yes, sir."

The master shook his head in resignation.

"You're quite beyond me, Morton," he said. "You have done a great many odd things since you've been in this school, but this is the oddest. Bringing a fish to school. Your lunch, indeed! Stay in for half an hour after school." Mr. Dowd sniffed. "And throw that fish out."

"Yes, sir."

Chet departed in disgrace, carrying the fish gingerly by the tail, while his classmates tried to stifle their laughter. Half way across the hall the unfortunate Chet met the principal, who spied the fish and demanded explanations. These not being satisfactory, he ordered Chet to write two hundred lines of Latin prose. By the time the jester returned to the classroom, after consigning the fish to the janitor, who put it carefully away with a view to taking it home so his wife could fry it for dinner, he was heartily regretting the impulse that had made him stop at the butcher shop. For the rest of the morning he was conscious of the smothered snickers of the Hardy boys and his chums.

Just before the recess period a note flicked onto his desk. He opened it and read: "He laughs best who laughs last."

Chet glared and looked back at Frank Hardy. But that youth was innocently engaged in his studies. There was a twinkle in his eye, however, that told better than words just who had written the note.

CHAPTER XII

The New Car

As days passed and the Shore Road mystery was no nearer solution, police activity was redoubled. Motorists became caustic in their comments and Chief Collig felt it as a reflection on his force that no clues had been unearthed.

The matter, however, was not wholly in the hands of the Bayport force, inasmuch as the Shore Road was beyond Chief Collig's jurisdiction, and the state troopers were also made aware of their responsibility. So, with local police, detectives and troopers on the case, it seemed that the auto thieves could scarcely hope to evade capture.

However, the search was in vain. Not a trace of the missing cars could be found. Even Fenton Hardy had to confess himself baffled.

"Looks as if there's a chance for us yet," said Frank Hardy.

"Looks to me as if there isn't. How can we hope to catch the auto thieves when every one else has fallen down on the job?" demanded his brother.

"We might be lucky. And, anyway, I've had an idea that might be worked out."

"What is it?"

"Come with me and I'll show you."

Mystified, Joe followed his brother out of the house and they went down the street in the direction of a well-known local automobile agency.

As they walked, Frank explained his plan. At first Joe was dubious.

"It couldn't be done."

"Why not? All we need is a little capital, and we have that. Then if we have nerve enough to go through with the rest of it, we may be lucky enough to trap the thieves."

"Too many 'ifs' and 'may bes' to suit me," demurred Joe. "Still, if you think we could get away with it, I'm with you."

"We may fail, but our money won't be altogether wasted. We've always wanted a car, anyway."

"That's true. We'll go and look this one over."

Arriving at the automobile agency, they were greeted by the manager, who knew them well.

"What is it this morning, boys?" he asked, with a smile. "Can I sell you a car to-day?"

He meant it as a joke, and he was greatly surprised when Frank answered:

"It all depends. We'll buy one if you can make us a good price."

"Why, that's fine," said the manager, immediately becoming businesslike. "What would you like to see? One of the new sport models?"

"No," replied Joe. "We're in the market for a used car."

"We heard you had Judge Keene's old car here," added Frank.

"Why, yes, we have. He turned it in and bought a new model. But you wouldn't want that car, boys. It looks like a million dollars, but it's all on the surface. I'll be frank with you—Judge Keene said the engine was no good, and I agree with him. It was put out by a new company that went bankrupt about a year later. They put all their money into the bodies of the cars and not very much into the engines. You would be wasting your money."

"We want a good-looking car, cheap," insisted Frank. "I don't care so much about the engine. It's the looks that count this time."

The manager shook his head.

"Well," he said, "I suppose you lads like to have a car that'll knock everybody's eye out, and I'm not denying this is a dandy-looking boat. But I won't guarantee its performance."

"We don't care, if the price is right. Where is it?"

The manager led the boys to the back of the showrooms, where they found a luxurious-looking auto. It looked, so Joe afterward said, "like a million dollars." With a fresh coat of paint it would have seemed like a model straight from the factory.

"What do you think of it?" Frank asked his brother.

"A peach."

"Boys, I hate to see you buy this car," the manager protested. "Take the money and put it into a good, standard car that you can depend on. You'll have more trouble running this automobile than the looks are worth. If you weren't friends of mine I wouldn't waste my time telling you this, for I'm anxious to get this mass of junk off my hands. But your father would never forgive me if he thought I'd stung you boys with a cement mixer like this one."

"It's the looks that count with us," said Frank. "How much do you want for it?"

"I'll sell it to you for four hundred dollars."

"Four hundred!" exclaimed Joe. "Why, that looks like a three-thousand-dollar car!"

"It looks like one, but it isn't," said the manager. "You'll be lucky to drive a thousand miles in it before the engine gives out."

"We won't drive any thousand miles in it," Joe remarked mysteriously.

"Don't let any one else have the car, and we'll go and get the money," Frank told the man.

They left the manager smoothing his hair and pondering on the folly of boys in general, although he was secretly relieved at having got rid of the imposing looking car, which he had regarded as a dead loss.

Going directly to the bank, the boys withdrew four hundred dollars from their account, after cautioning the teller not to mention the matter to their father.

"We're going to give him a little surprise," said Frank.

"All right," said the teller, wondering what the boys wanted with such a large sum, "I won't tell him."

Back to the agency they went, handed over the money, and drove out in state, Frank at the wheel of their new possession. The car was indeed a splendid-looking vehicle, having excellent lines, good fittings, and a quantity of nickel trimmings that enhanced its luxurious appearance. Frank soon found that the manager had spoken correctly when he said that the value was all on the surface, for the engine began giving trouble before they had driven two blocks.

"However," he said to his brother, "this old boat may earn us a lot more than the money we paid for it, and if it doesn't we'll have plenty of fun tinkering around and putting a real engine in it."

They drove into the yard of their home. Aunt Gertrude spied them first and uttered a squawk of astonishment, then fled into the house to inform Mrs. Hardy of this latest evidence of imbecility on the part of the lads. Their mother came out, and the boys admitted that the car was theirs.

"We're not extravagant, Mother," they protested. "We got it for a certain reason, and we'll tell you all about it later. The old boat isn't as expensive as it looks. We picked it up cheap."

Mrs. Hardy had implicit confidence in her sons and when they said there was a reason behind the purchase she was content to bide her time and await their explanations. She was curious to know why they had made this extraordinary move, but was too discreet to ask any questions.

With the car in the garage, the boys went downtown again and bought several cans of automobile paint. And, for the rest of the week, they busied themselves transforming the automobile into "a thing of beauty and a joy forever."

Their parents were puzzled, but said nothing. Aunt Gertrude was frankly indignant and at mealtimes made many veiled references to the luxury-loving tendencies of modern youth.

"It's not enough for them to have motorcycles and a motorboat, but now they must have an automobile!" she sniffed. "And it's not enough for them to buy an ordinary flivver—they must have a car that a millionaire would be proud to own."

Secretly, the boys considered this a compliment. They felt that their aunt would be vastly surprised if she knew the low price they had paid.

"Wait till she sees it when we have it painted," said Frank.

Their chums, too, were unable to imagine what had possessed the Hardy boys to purchase a so large and expensive-looking car. Frank and Joe did not enlighten them. They had bought the car for a certain purpose and they were afraid that if they confided in any one, their plans might leak out. So they busied themselves with painting the new car, and said nothing of their intentions to any one, not even to Chet Morton.

At last the work was finished.

On Friday night after school Frank applied the last dab of paint, and the brothers stood back to survey their handiwork.

"She's a beauty!" declared Joe.

"I'll tell the world!"

The automobile was resplendent in its fresh coat of paint. The nickel glittered.

"Looks like a Rolls-Royce."

"A car like that would tempt any auto thief in the world."

"I hope it does."

"Well, we're all set for Act Two," said Frank. "I think we'll go out to-night. Our bait is ready."

"I hope we catch something."

With this mysterious dialogue, the boys went into the house for supper.

They were so excited over their impending journey that they could scarcely take time to eat.

"Some mischief on foot," commented Aunt Gertrude.

CHAPTER XIII

In the Locker

The massive roadster rolled smoothly out of the garage that evening and the Hardy boys drove down High Street, greatly enjoying the attention their new car attracted. Freshly painted, the automobile had not the slightest evidence of being a second-hand car. It was long and low-slung, with a high hood, and there was a big locker at the back.

The upholstery was in good condition and the fittings were ornate and handsome. All in all, it was a car to arouse the envy of all their chums, and one that would arouse the covetousness of any auto thief.

This was precisely what the Hardy boys were counting on.

They drove about the streets until it was almost dark. They met Biff Hooper and Tony Prito, who exclaimed over the luxurious appearance of the roadster and immediately wanted a ride, but the boys were obliged to refuse.

"Sorry," said Frank. "We'll take you out any other time but to-night. We have business in hand."

"I'd like to know what it's all about," remarked Biff. "You two have been mighty mysterious about something lately."

"Some time you'll understand," sang out Joe, as they drove off.

They headed out the Shore Road.

It was getting dark and the headlights cut a brilliant slash through the gloom.

Leaving Bayport behind, the boys drove about two miles out until they came to a place where a grassy meadow beside the road provided a favorite parking place for motorists who wished to descend the path leading down through the woods to the beach below.

"This is about as good a place as any," said Frank.

"Suits me."

He drove the car off the road onto the grass. It came to a stop.

"Any one around, Joe?"

Joe looked back.

"No other cars in sight," he reported a moment later.

"Then make it snappy."

Any one observing the roadster at that moment would have seen the two boys clamber out, but in the gloom they would not have seen what followed. For the boys suddenly disappeared.

The roadster remained where it was, parked by the road, in solitary magnificence. A few minutes later an automobile passed by. It belonged to a Bayport merchant, out for an evening drive. He saw the splendid car by the roadside and said to his wife:

"Somebody is taking an awful chance. I wouldn't leave a fine-looking automobile like that out here without some one to watch it. I guess the owner is down on the beach. If one of those auto thieves happens along there'll be another good car listed among the missing."

"Well, it's their own lookout," returned his wife.

They drove past.

But the roadster was not deserted, as it seemed. So quickly had the Hardy boys concealed themselves that, even had any one been watching, it would have been difficult to follow their movements.

The roadster, having been built for show, had a large and roomy locker at the back. By experimenting in the privacy of the garage and by clearing this locker of all odds and ends, the boys found it was just large enough to accommodate them both. Here they were hidden. They were not uncomfortable, and the darkness did not bother them, for each was equipped with a small flashlight.

"You didn't forget your revolver, did you?" whispered Frank.

"No. I have it here," answered his brother. "Have you got yours?"

"Ready in case I need it."

Although there would seem to be no purpose in spending an evening crouched in the locker of a parked roadster, the Hardy boys had laid definite plans. From the morning they had bought the car they had perfected the various details of their scheme to capture the auto thieves on the Shore Road.

"Most of the cars have been stolen while they were parked on the Shore Road," Frank had argued. "It stands to reason that the auto thieves are operating along there. Since the first few scares, not many people have been parking their cars along there, so the thieves have taken to stealing cars in town and to hold-ups. If we park the roadster, it's ten chances to one the thieves won't be able to resist the temptation."

"And we lose a perfectly good car," objected Joe.

"We won't lose it, because we'll be right in it all the time."

"The thieves won't be likely to steal it if we're in it."

"They won't see us. We'll be hiding in the locker."

Joe saw the merits of the plan at once.

"And they'll kidnap us without knowing it?" he chuckled.

"That's the idea. They'll drive the car to wherever they are in the habit of hiding the stolen autos, and then we can watch our chance to either round them up then and there or else steal away and come back with the police."

This, then, was the explanation of their mysterious behavior, and as they crouched in the locker they were agog with expectation.

"We'll just have to be patient," whispered Frank, when they had been in hiding for more than half an hour. "Can't expect the fish to bite the minute we put out the bait."

Joe settled himself into a more comfortable position.

"This is the queerest fishing *I've* ever done," he mused.

It was very quiet. They had no difficulty in breathing, as the locker had a number of air spaces that they had bored in the top and sides, invisible to a casual glance.

Once in a while they could hear a car speeding past on the Shore Road.

Minute after minute went by. They were becoming cramped. Presently Joe yawned loud and long.

"I guess it's no use," said Frank, at last. "We're out of luck to-night."

"Can't expect to be lucky the first time," replied his brother philosophically.

"We might as well go home."

Frank raised the lid of the locker and peeped out. It was quite dark. The Shore Road was deserted.

"Coast is clear," he said.

They got quickly out of the locker. They lost no time, for there was a possibility that one of the auto thieves might be in the neighborhood, watching the roadster, and if their trap was discovered it would be useless to make a second attempt.

They got back into the car, Joe taking the wheel this time. He drove the roadster back onto the highway, turned it around, and they set out back for Bayport.

Both lads were disappointed, although they had not yet given up hope. They had been so confident that their plan would be successful that this failure took some of the wind out of their sails, so to speak.

"We'll just try again to-morrow night," said Frank.

"Perhaps the auto thieves have quit."

"Not them! They'll fall for our trap yet."

"I'm glad we didn't tell any of the fellows. We'll look mighty foolish if it doesn't work."

The car sped along the Shore Road, the headlights casting a brilliant beam of illumination. As they rounded a curve they caught a glimpse of a dark figure trudging along in the shadow of the trees bordering the ditch.

"Wonder who that is," Frank remarked, peering at the man.

Joe bore down on the wheel, swinging the car around so that the headlights fell full on the man beside the road. Then he swung the car back into its course again.

The fellow had flung up his arm to shield his face from the glare, but he had not been quick enough to hide his features altogether. Frank had recognized him at once.

"So!" he remarked thoughtfully. "Our friend again."

"I didn't get a good look at him," Joe said. "Somehow, he seemed familiar."

"He was. I'd recognize that face anywhere now."

"Who was it?"

"Gus Montrose."

Joe whistled.

"I wonder what he's doing, skulking along here at this time of night."

"I have an idea that we'll find out before long."

"Do you think he has anything to do with the car thefts?"

"Shouldn't be surprised. He seems a rather suspicious sort of character."

They sped past the dark figure, who went on, head down, hands thrust deep in his coat pockets.

"I'd like to know more about that chap," mused Frank. "I'll bet he's not hanging around here for any good reason."

CHAPTER XIV

Montrose Again

The Hardy boys were not discouraged by this failure. They realized that it was too much to hope for success in their venture at the first trial and resolved to lay their trap again.

If their parents were curious as to why they had remained out so late, they gave no sign of it, and the following night Frank and Joe, again drove out along the Shore Road in their new car. This time they went to another parking place, not far from the spot where Isaac Fussy's automobile had been stolen.

Again they turned out the lights, again they crawled into the locker at the back, and again they remained in hiding, while car after car went by on the Shore Road.

An hour passed.

"Looks as if we're out of luck again," whispered Joe.

"We'll stay with it a while longer."

Frank switched on his flashlight and glanced at his watch. It was almost ten o'clock. They heard an automobile roar past at tremendous speed, and a few moments later there was the heavy rumble of a truck.

"Funny time of night for a truck to be out," Frank remarked.

"That first car was sure breaking all speed laws."

After a long time, Frank again looked at his watch.

"Half-past ten."

"Another evening wasted."

"Are you getting tired?"

"My legs are so cramped I don't think I'll ever be able to walk straight again."

Joe had inadvertently raised his voice. Suddenly Frank gripped his arm.

"Shh!"

They listened. They heard footsteps coming along the road. The steps sounded clear and distinct on the hard highway. Then they became soft and muffled as the pedestrian turned out onto the grassy slope.

"Coming this way," whispered Frank.

Some one approached the roadster cautiously. The boys could hear him moving around the car. After a moment or so, one of the doors was opened and some one clambered into the seat.

The boys were breathless with excitement. Was this one of the auto thieves?

But the intruder made no move to drive the car away. Instead, when he had snapped the lights on and off, he got out, closed the door behind him and strode off through the grass.

The first impulse of the two brothers was to clamber out, but they realized that this would be folly. They remained quiet, as the footsteps receded into the distance. The man gained the road again and walked slowly away. Finally, they heard the footsteps no more.

Frank sighed with disappointment.

"I thought sure we had a bite that time," he said.

"It was only a nibble."

When the lads were quite sure their unknown visitor had gone, Frank raised the lid of the locker and the boys got out.

"I guess it was only some farmer on the way home. He probably just got into the car out of curiosity."

"He wasn't an auto thief, that's certain, or he would have driven off with it."

"Not much use staying around any longer."

They got back into the seat. Nothing had been disturbed. Beyond turning the lights on and off, the stranger had tampered with nothing.

Frank started up the engine, and drove the car back onto the Shore Road. There was not much room in which to turn around, so he drove on down the road for about a quarter of a mile until he came to a lane which offered sufficient space.

Just as he was bringing the car around to head back toward Bayport, the headlights shone on two figures coming up the road. In the glare, the men were clearly revealed.

"There's our friend Gus again," remarked Frank quietly.

He was right. There was no mistaking the surly visage of the ex-farmhand. The man with him was unknown to the boys, but he was no more prepossessing than his companion. Broad of build, unshaven of face, he was not the sort of fellow one would care to meet alone on a dark night.

"Handsome-looking pair," Joe commented.

The car swung out into the road and the two men stepped out into the ditch, turning their faces away. Frank stepped on the accelerator, and the roadster shot ahead.

"This seems to be Gus Montrose's beat," he said, when they had driven beyond hearing distance.

"Wonder what takes him out alone; here every night."

"Perhaps he was the chap who got into the roadster."

But Frank shook his head.

"That fellow went away in the direction Montrose is coming from," he pointed out, "And, besides, he was alone."

"That's true, too."

Wondering what brought Montrose and his villainous-looking companion out the Shore Road on foot at that hour, the Hardy boys drove back into Bayport.

"Better luck next time," said Frank, cheering up.

"We won't give up yet. Third time's lucky you know."

"Let's hope so. To-morrow night may tell."

They drove back into the city without incident, and when they reached their home they saw that there was a light in their father's study. Frank's face lengthened.

"I'll bet we're in for it now. He doesn't often stay up this late."

"He's likely sitting up to lecture us."

They put the car into the garage. The light in the study seemed ominous just then.

"Well," said Joe, "I guess we might as well go in and face the music. If the worst comes to the worst we'll tell him just what we were up to."

They went into the house. It would have been easy for them to have gained their room by the back stairs, but the boys had too much principle to dodge any unpleasantness in this manner, so they made a point of passing by their father's study. The door was open and they saw Fenton Hardy sitting at his desk. He was not writing, but was gazing in front of him with a fixed expression on his face. A telephone was at his elbow.

To their relief, he smiled when he saw them.

"Come in," he invited.

Frank and Joe entered the study.

"Did you catch any auto thieves?" asked their father.

The boys were astonished.

"How did you know we were after auto thieves, Dad?" asked Frank.

"It doesn't take a great deal of perception to find that out," their father answered. "All these mysterious doings can have only one reason."

"Well, we didn't catch any," Joe admitted.

"I didn't think so. They've been busy to-night."

"Again!"

Fenton Hardy nodded.

"I've just been talking to the secretary of the Automobile Club. He telephoned me a short time ago. The thieves cut loose in earnest this evening."

"Did they steal another car?"

"Two. They made off with a new Buick that was parked down on Oak Street, and then they stole a truck from one of the wholesale companies."

"Can you beat that!" breathed Joe. "Two more gone!"

"They were taken within a few minutes of each other, evidently. The reports reached the police station almost at the same time. The truck mightn't have been missed until morning, but one of the wholesale company employees was coming home and he recognized it as it was driven away. He thought it rather suspicious, so he went on up to the company garage and found the truck had disappeared."

The brothers looked at one another.

"A truck and a pleasure car!" exclaimed Frank. "Why, that must have been—"

The same thought had struck Joe.

"The two cars that passed us on the Shore Road! What time were they stolen, Dad?"

"Some time between half-past nine and ten o'clock. Why? Did you see them?"

"Two cars went out the Shore Road a little before ten o'clock. They were both going at a fast clip. I remember we remarked at the time that it was a funny hour of the night for a truck to be out."

"The Shore Road, eh? Did you get a good look at them?"

The boys were embarrassed.

"Well, to tell the truth," said Frank hesitatingly, "we didn't exactly see them. We heard them."

"Hm! You didn't see them, but you heard them, and you were on the Shore Road. That's a little mystery in itself," remarked their father, with a smile.

He reached for the telephone and asked for a number. In a short time his party answered.

"Hello, Chief. This is Fenton Hardy speaking. . . . Yes. . . . I've just had information that the big car and the truck went out the Shore Road way a few minutes before ten o'clock. . . . Yes. . . . You've made inquiries? . . . I see. . . . That's strange, isn't it? . . . Yes, my information is quite reliable. . . . All right. . . . Let me know if you hear anything. . . . Don't mention it. . . . Thank you, Chief. . . . Good-bye."

He put down the telephone.

"I was talking to Chief Collig. He says the three towns at the other end of the Shore Road were notified immediately after the thefts were discovered and that they had officers watching the roads from ten o'clock on."

"And they didn't see the cars?"

Fenton Hardy shook his head.

"Not the slightest trace of either of them."

Frank and Joe looked at one another blankly.

"Well, if that don't beat the Dutch!" Frank exclaimed.

"You're quite sure of the time?"

"Positive. I had just looked at my watch."

"Well," said Fenton Hardy, "since the cars haven't been seen in any of the other towns and since there aren't any other roads, the Shore Road must hold the solution. I think I'll do a little prospecting around the farms out that way to-morrow."

"We've been doing a little prospecting ourselves," admitted Joe, "but we haven't been very successful so far."

"Keep at it," their father said encouragingly. "And good luck to you both!"

CHAPTER XV

The Suspect

It was late before the Hardy boys got to sleep that night.

The events of the evening, culminating in the discovery that the auto thieves had been at work in Bayport while they were lying in wait for them on the Shore Road, gave the lads plenty to talk about before they were finally claimed by slumber.

In the morning, it required two calls to arouse them. They dressed sleepily and had to hurry downstairs in order to be in time for breakfast. This did not escape the notice of ever-watchful Aunt Gertrude.

"When *I* was a girl," she said pointedly, "young people went to bed at a reasonable hour and didn't go gallivanting all over the country half the night. Every growing boy and girl needs eight or nine hours' sleep. I'd be ashamed to come down to breakfast rubbing my eyes and gaping."

"It isn't very often they get up late," said Mrs. Hardy. "We can overlook it once in a while, I suppose."

"Overlook it!" snorted Aunt Gertrude. "Mark my words, Laura, those boys will come to no good end if you encourage them in coming in at all hours of the night. Goodness knows what mischief they were up to." She glared severely at them.

Frank and Joe realized that their aunt was curious as to where they had been the past two evenings and was using this roundabout method of tempting them into an explanation. However, as Joe expressed it later, they "refused to bite."

Instead, they hastily consumed their breakfast, drawing from the good lady a lecture on the dreadful consequences of eating in a hurry, illustrated by an anecdote concerning a little boy named Hector, who met a lamentable and untimely death by choking himself on a piece of steak and passed away surrounded by weeping relatives.

The boys, however, were evidently not impressed by the fate of the unfortunate Hector, for they gulped down their meal, snatched up their books, and rushed off to school without waiting for Aunt Gertrude's account of the funeral. They were crossing the school yard when the bell rang and they reached the classroom just in time.

"I feel like a stewed owl," was Joe's comment.

"Never ate stewed owl," returned his brother promptly. "How does it taste?"

"I said I felt, I didn't say I ate," retorted Joe. "Gee, but your eyes do look bunged up."

"What about your own?"

"Oh, if only I had had just one more hour's sleep!"

"I could go two or three."

"Aunt Gertrude was onto us."

"Yes, but she didn't get anywhere with it."

"Hope I don't fall asleep over my desk."

"Same here."

The morning dragged. They were very sleepy. Once or twice, Joe yawned openly and Miss Petty, who taught history, accused him of lack of interest in the proceedings.

"You may keep yourself awake by telling us what you know of the Roman system of government under Julius Cæsar," she said.

Joe got to his feet. He floundered through a more or less acceptable account of Roman government. It was dreary stuff, and Frank, listening to the droning voice, became drowsier and drowsier. His head nodded, and finally he went to sleep altogether and had a vivid dream in which he chased Julius Cæsar, attired in a toga and with a laurel wreath on his head, along the Shore Road in a steam-roller.

Miss Petty left the Romans and began comparing ancient and modern systems of government, which led her into a discourse on the life of Abraham Lincoln. She was just reaching Lincoln's death when there was a loud snore.

Miss Petty looked up.

"Who made that noise?"

Another snore.

Joe dug his brother in the ribs with a ruler and Frank looked up, with an expression of surprise on his face.

"Frank Hardy, are you paying attention?"

"Yes, ma'am," replied Frank, now wide awake. In his dream he imagined Julius Cæsar had turned on him and had poked him in the ribs with a spear.

"Do you know who we were talking about?"

"Oh, yes, ma'am."

"Do you know anything about his death?"

"Yes, ma'am," said Frank, under the impression that the lesson still dealt with Cæsar.

"How did he die?"

"He was stabbed."

"He was stabbed, was he? Where?"

"In—in the Forum. He was murdered by some of the senators, led by Cassius and Brutus, and Marc Antony made a speech."

The class could contain itself no longer. Snickers burst out, and these welled into a wave of laughter in which even Miss Petty was forced to join. Frank looked around in vast surprise.

"This," said the teacher, "is an interesting fact about Lincoln. I don't remember having heard of it before. So he was stabbed to death by the senators and Marc Antony made a speech?"

"I—I was talking about Cæsar, Miss Petty."

"And *I* was talking about Abraham Lincoln. Will you be good enough to stay awake for the remainder of the lesson, Hardy?"

Frank looked sheepishly at his book, while Chet Morton doubled up in his seat and gave vent to a series of explosive chuckles that soon brought the teacher's attention to him and he was required to recite the Gettysburg Address, stalling completely before he had gone a dozen words. By the time the teacher had finished her comments on his poor memory, Chet had other things to occupy his mind. Frank and Joe Hardy were wide awake for the rest of the morning.

After lunch, they were on their way back to school, resolving to cut out the late hours, so as not to risk a repetition of the ridicule they had suffered that morning, when Frank suddenly caught sight of a familiar figure not far ahead.

"Why, there's Gus Montrose again," he said. "Wonder what he's doing in town?"

"Let's trail him," Joe suggested.

"Good idea. We'll find out what he does with his time."

The former hired man of the Dodds was shambling down the street at a lazy gait, apparently wrapped up in his own concerns. Frank and Joe followed, at a respectful distance. When Montrose reached a busy corner he turned down a side street and here his demeanor changed. His shoulders were straighter and his step more purposeful.

Taking the opposite side of the street, the boys strolled along, keeping well behind Montrose but not letting him out of sight. They followed him for about two blocks and then, leaning against a telegraph pole at the next corner, they saw Montrose's companion of the previous night. He looked up as Montrose approached, and then the pair met and joined in earnest conversation.

There was something peculiarly furtive about the two men. Not wishing to be observed, the Hardy boys stepped into a soft drink place near by and bought some ginger ale, which they drank in the store, keeping an eye on the pair across the street, through the window.

Finally, Montrose's companion moved slowly away, and Montrose himself shambled across the road. He was lost to sight for a moment.

"We'll trail him a little while longer," said Frank. "We have about a quarter of an hour before school opens."

They paid for the ginger ale and stepped out of the shop. To their astonishment, Gus Montrose was coming directly toward them. They had lost sight of him in the window and had assumed that he had gone on down the street. Instead he had turned back.

They affected not to notice him, and were starting back up the street when Montrose overtook them and brushed against Frank rudely.

"Look here," he said, in a gruff voice. "What's the idea of followin' me, hey?"

"Following you!" said Frank, in tones of simulated surprise.

"Yes—followin' me. I saw you. What do you mean by it?"

"Can't we walk down the same street?" inquired Joe.

"You didn't walk down here by accident. You followed me here."

"You must have something on your conscience if you think that," Frank told him. "This is a free country. We can walk where we like."

"Is that so? Well, I'm not goin' to put up with havin' a pair of young whippersnappers trailin' *me* around town," snarled Gus Montrose. "Hear that?"

"We hear you."

"Well, remember it, then. You just mind your own business after this, see?"

"If you think we were following you, that's your own affair," returned Frank. "We're on our way to school, if you'd like to know."

"Well, see that you go there. You're better off in school than monkeyin' in my affairs, let me tell you. And a sight safer, too."

The man's tone was truculent.

"Oh, I think you're pretty harmless," laughed Joe.

"You'll find out how harmless I am if I catch you followin' me around again. Just mind your own business after this and keep goin' in the opposite direction when you see me comin'."

The man's insulting tone annoyed Frank.

"Look here," he said, sharply, facing Montrose. "If you don't start off in the opposite direction right now, I'll call a policeman. Now, get out of here."

Somewhat taken aback, Gus Montrose halted.

"You were followin' me—" he growled.

"You heard what I said. Clear out of here and stop annoying us."

If Montrose had hoped to frighten the lads, he was disappointed. Like most cowardly men, he backed down readily when confronted with opposition.

Grumbling to himself, he turned away and crossed the street.

The Hardy boys went on toward school.

"That'll give him something to think about," remarked Frank.

"You hit the right note when you said he must have something on his conscience or he wouldn't have thought we were following him."

"I'm sure he has. A man with a clear conscience would never suspect he was being trailed. There's something mighty fishy about Gus Montrose and his queer-looking friend."

"Too bad he saw us. He'll be on his guard against us now."

"That doesn't matter. We can keep an eye on him just the same. I'd give a farm to know what the pair of them were talking about."

"And I'd give a five-dollar bill just to know if he put that fishing pole in the car up at the Dodds' and got Jack into trouble."

"So would I."

The boys were greatly puzzled. They were convinced that Gus Montrose was up to no good and this conviction had only been strengthened by their encounter. They reasoned that a law-abiding man would scarcely have shown such resentment as Montrose had evidenced.

"Well, whether he's one of the thieving party or not, we'll take another whirl at the Shore Road to-night," said Frank, as the two brothers entered the school yard.

Joe glanced at the sky. Massed clouds were gathering and the air was close.

"Looks as if we'll have to call it off. There's going to be a storm."

"Storm or no storm, I have a hunch that we'll get some action before the day is out."

Both Frank and Joe were right.

There was a storm, and before midnight they had more action than they had ever bargained for.

CHAPTER XVI

Kidnaped

Rain threatened throughout the afternoon, but although the sky darkened and there was an ominous calm, the storm held off. After supper the Hardy boys went outside and looked at the clouds.

"It's sure going to be a jim-dandy," declared Joe. "Do you think we really should go out to-night?"

"A little thing like a storm won't hold the car thieves back. They'll operate in any weather."

"Won't they think it queer to see a car parked out in the rain?"

"They'll probably think it was stalled and that the owner went to get help."

"That's right, too," Joe agreed. "I guess we can chance it."

"We'll put the top up to protect ourselves. And, anyway, it's dry in the locker."

"The rain will be the least of our worries in there," said Joe, with a grin. "Let's be going."

They went out to the garage and put up the top of the roadster, then got in. As they drove down High Street there was a low rumble of thunder and a splash of rain against the windshield.

"Storm's coming, right enough," Frank said. "Still, I have a hunch."

Ever since the previous night he had been possessed by a feeling that their next venture would be crowned with success. He could not explain it, but the feeling was there nevertheless.

They spied Con Riley, in oilskins against the approaching downpour, patrolling his beat, and drew up at the curb.

"New car, eh?" said Riley, surveying the roadster grimly. "I'll be runnin' you in for speeding some of these days, I'll be bound."

"Not in this boat," Frank assured him. "If we ever hit higher than thirty the engine would fly out."

"Thirty!" scoffed the constable. "That looks like a real racin' car. You mean ninety."

"We'll take you for a drive some time when you're off duty. We just stopped to ask if there was anything new about the auto thieves."

Riley looked very grave, as he always did when any one asked him questions pertaining to police matters.

"Well," he said, "there is and there isn't."

"That mean's there isn't."

"We ain't found 'em yet. But that don't mean they won't be found," said the officer darkly. "We're followin' up clues."

"What kind of clues?"

"Oh, just clues," said the officer vaguely. "We'll have 'em behind the bars before long. But you'd better keep an eye on that car of yours. It's just the kind somebody would steal."

"Trust us. There's been no trace of the other cars, then?"

Riley shook his head.

"Not a sign. But them thieves will go too far some of these fine days, and then we'll catch 'em."

"Well, we hope you're the man who lands them," said Frank cheerfully, as he edged the car out from the curb again. "So long."

The boys drove away, and Con Riley patiently resumed his beat.

"The game is still open," remarked Joe. "If the police had learned anything new, Riley would have heard about it."

"Whenever he says they're following up clues, you can be certain that they're up against it. The thieves are just as much at large as they ever were."

It was beginning to rain heavily before they reached the outskirts of Bayport and by the time they were well out on the Shore Road the storm was upon them. Thunder rolled and rumbled in the blackening sky and jagged streaks of lightning flickered through the clouds. Rain streamed down in the glare of the headlights.

As the downpour grew in violence, the road became more treacherous. Without chains, the rear wheels of the car skidded and slithered on the greasy surface.

One of the numerous defects of the roadster's mechanism was a loose steering wheel. Under ordinary circumstances it gave little trouble, but on this treacherous road, Frank experienced difficulty in keeping the car on its course.

Just outside Bayport was a steep hill, dipping to the bluffs that overhung the bay. Under the influence of the rain, the sloping road had become wet and sticky, and as the roadster began the descent Frank knew he was in for trouble.

The car skidded wildly, and the faulty brakes did not readily respond. Once, the nose of the roadster appeared to be heading directly toward the steep bluff, where only a narrow ledge separated the boys from a terrible plunge onto the rocks of the beach below. Joe gave a gasp of apprehension, but Frank bore down on the wheel and managed to swing the car back onto the road again in the nick of time.

But the danger was not yet over.

The car was tobogganing down the slope as though entirely out of control. The rear wheels skidded crazily and several times the car was almost directly across the road, sliding sideways, and when it did regain the ruts it shot ahead with breath-taking speed.

Almost any second the boys expected the roadster would leave the slippery clay and either shoot across the ledge into space or crash into the rocky wall at the left.

Somehow, luck was with them. Luck and Frank's quick work at the unreliable wheel saved them from disaster.

The car gained the level ground, settled into the ruts, and went speeding on at a more reasonable rate. The lads now breathed more easily.

"Looked like our finish, that time," observed Joe.

"I'll say it did! I wouldn't have given a nickel for our chances when we were about half way down the hill."

"Well, a miss is as good as a mile. We're still alive."

"And the old boat is still rolling along. When we get back I'm going to have that steering wheel fixed. It very nearly cost us our lives."

On through the storm the Hardy boys drove, until at last they reached the place where they had parked on the previous night. There was no one in sight as they drove out onto the grass, and Frank turned off the engine and switched out the lights. Quickly, they scrambled out, raised the lid of the locker, and got inside.

The locker was warm and dry. The boys were comfortable enough, aside from being somewhat cramped, and they could hear the rain roaring down on the top of the roadster as the storm grew in violence.

Warned by their former experience, the boys had made themselves more comfortable than they had previously been. On the floor of the locker they had spread a soft rug and they had also supplied themselves with two small but comfortable pillows.

"I am not going to wear out my knees and elbows," Frank had said. "The last time we were out my left elbow was black and blue."

"We'll fix it up as comfortable as a bed," Joe had answered.

In addition to the rug and pillows the boys had brought along a small box of fancy crackers and also a bottle of cold water, for hiding in the locker for hours had made them both hungry and thirsty.

"I could eat a few crackers right now," remarked Joe, shortly after they had settled down to their vigil.

"Same here," answered his brother. "Pass the box over."

Each lad had several crackers and followed them with a swallow of water. As they munched the crackers the thunder rolled and rolled in the distance and they could see an occasional flash of lightning through a crack of the locker door.

"It sure is a dirty night," Frank whispered, is they crouched in the darkness of their voluntary prison.

"Even for auto thieves."

Thunder rolled and grumbled and the rain poured down in drenching torrents. They could hear the beating of the surf on the distant shore of Barmet Bay, far below.

Minutes passed, with only the monotonous roar of the storm.

"What's the time?" asked Joe finally.

Frank switched on the flashlight and glanced at his watch.

"Half-past nine."

"Time enough yet."

They settled down to wait. Scarcely five minutes had passed before they heard a new sound above the clamor of the rain and wind.

Some one stepped up on the running board of the roadster, flung open the door, and sat down behind the wheel. The boys had not heard the intruder's approach, owing to the noise of the storm, and they sat up, startled.

The newcomer lost no time.

In a moment, the engine roared, and then the car started forward with a jerk.

It lurched across the grassy ground, then climbed up onto the Shore Road. Back in the locker, the lads were bounced and jolted against one another. They did not mind this, for there was wild joy in their hearts. At last their patient vigil had been rewarded.

"Kidnaped!" whispered Frank exultantly.

Once on the road, the car set off at rapidly increasing speed through the storm. The man at the wheel was evidently an expert driver, for he got every ounce of power the engine was capable of, and held the roadster to the highway. The roar of the motor could be heard high above the drumming of the rain.

In the darkness of the locker, the boys sat tight, not knowing where the car was going, not knowing how long this wild journey might last. They kept alert for any turns from the Shore Road, realizing that they might have to find their way back by memory.

For above five minutes, the car held to the Shore Road, and then suddenly swerved to the right.

Neither of the boys had any recollection of a side road in this part of the country, and they were immediately surprised. However, by the violent lurching and jolting of the roadster they were soon aware that they were on no traveled thoroughfare and that they were descending a slope over rough ground. There was a loud swishing of branches and the sharp snapping of twigs, that indicated the roadster was passing through the woods.

The man at the wheel was driving more carefully now that he was off the Shore Road and comparatively safe from observation. He was evidently following a road of sorts, although the car swerved and jolted unmercifully, but at length he came to even more precarious ground.

The rear of the roadster went high in the air and came down with a crash. Frank and Joe were flung violently to the bottom of the locker, and Frank felt a most stunning blow on the head.

Thud!

Another terrific jolt. The car pitched and tossed like a ship in a storm.

Bang!

A tire had blown out.

But this did not appear to worry the driver. The car canted far over on one side, lurched forward, and then came down on all four wheels with a terrific impact.

The boys were badly shaken up. They tried to brace themselves against the sides of the locker, but this was of little use as the roadster's bumpy and erratic progress inevitably dislodged them. They were thrown against one another, bounced from side to side, bruised and battered.

It was apparent to them that the roadster was being driven over some rocks—not the boulders of the beach, but over a rocky section of ground where there was no road.

They shielded their heads with their arms as well as they could, to prevent themselves from being knocked senseless against the sides of the locker. The speed of the car slackened. Then they felt a long series of short, sharp bumps, as though the car were being driven over pebbles. Stones banged against the mudguards.

"We're on the beach," reflected Frank.

They did not suffer the jouncing and jolting that had given them such discomfort a short time previously. The car traveled along the beach for a short distance, then turned to the left and ran quietly and smoothly over what the boys judged to be a stretch of sand. It then began to climb. The ascent flung the lads against the back of the locker.

It was of short duration, however.

The roadster came to level ground again, then rattled and rumbled on over an uneven surface.

The boys noticed a peculiar, hollow sound. The roar of the motor seemed to be echoing from all sides. The car had slowed down, and at last it came to a stop. Battered and bruised, the lads crouched in their hiding place, wondering what would happen next. They could hear the driver scrambling out of the front seat. Then there was a voice:

"That, you, Alex?"

"Yep."

"What have you got?"

"Big roadster."

"The one we were talking about?"

"You bet."

Other voices followed, voices that echoed and re-echoed, and then footsteps clattered on rock.

"A beauty!" exclaimed some one. "Have any trouble?"

"None at all," said the voice of the man who had been addressed as Alex. "Nobody in sight, so I just hopped in and drove it out."

"Swell boat!" declared some one else. "Fine night to leave it out in the rain."

"That's what I thought," said Alex. "So I drove it in out of the wet."

There was a general laugh. From the number of voices, the lads judged that there were at least three or four men standing near the big car.

"Wonder who owns it," said one of the several men.

"I don't know who *did* own it, but I know that *we* own it now," answered Alex promptly.

"What'll we do? Leave it here?"

"There isn't room inside. Might as well leave it."

"I guess nobody will come along and steal it," remarked Alex, who was evidently the wit of the party, for another burst of laughter greeted his words. "Want to look the car over?" he asked.

"Oh, it looks good enough from here."

"What's in that locker?" said one of the men. "There might be something valuable."

A thrill of fear went through the two boys.

One of the men approached the back of the car. Frank gripped his revolver firmly.

CHAPTER XVII

The Cave

In a moment the lid of the locker would have been raised.

Then came an interruption.

"The boss wants us," said one of the men.

The man approaching the back of the car halted.

"All right," he growled. "We'll leave this."

He turned away. The Hardy boys sighed with relief.

"I guess he's waitin' for a report," observed a voice, as the men began to move off. Their footsteps sounded sharp and clear on the rocks.

The sounds died away.

Complete silence prevailed. Not even a murmur broke the stillness. The lads remained quiet in the darkness of their hiding place.

Finally Frank stirred.

"They've gone," he whispered.

"What shall we do now?" asked Joe.

"Let's get out of here first. They may come back at any minute."

Frank raised the lid cautiously. The blackness without was as utter and complete as the darkness within. He could see nothing.

He listened for a moment, thinking possibly some of the gang had remained behind, but he heard nothing. Quickly, he got out of the locker and leaped to the ground. Joe followed. They closed the lid.

"Boy! I thought it was all up with us," whispered Joe. "When he came over to open the locker my heart was thumping so loudly I was sure he could hear it."

"Me, too. Well, we can thank their boss—whoever he is. I wonder what kind of place we're in, anyway."

Frank switched on his flashlight.

By its brilliant gleam, he saw that they were in a rocky passageway, a large tunnel evidently in the bluffs along Barmet Bay. It was wide enough to accommodate the roadster, but did not offer a great deal of leeway on either side. It appeared to be a natural tunnel, although there was evidence that human toil had been responsible for widening it and clearing it out.

Frank stepped forward and cast the ray of light before him.

It revealed a blank wall of rock. Then, as he moved the flashlight to one side he saw that the tunnel slanted toward the left.

"What'll we do!" asked Joe. "Follow it up along?"

He spoke in a whisper, but the walls magnified his voice and he awakened uncanny echoes.

"Sure. We'll have to be careful, though, or we might meet them on the way back."

Frank took the lead. He stepped forward very carefully, making no move that might dislodge a loose fragment of rock and start a tumult of echoes that would bring the gang upon them.

Cautiously, they advanced. Joe took his revolver from his pocket and gripped it tightly.

They realized that they were dealing with a band of desperate men, who would stop at nothing if they were discovered.

The Hardy boys rounded the corner of the passageway, and Frank's flashlight revealed a number of large boxes, stacked up against the side of the tunnel. They halted and Frank scrutinized some lettering on the boxes.

"The Eastern Importing Company," he read.

"Why, that's the name of the company that lost the truck!" Joe exclaimed.

"Remember? The two men who were held up and rolled down the bluff."

"It's the same name, all right. I'll bet this is some of the truck cargo."

The boxes were seven in number, and on each was inscribed the name of the Eastern Importing Company.

There was no doubt in the minds of the Hardy boys now that they had made a momentous discovery. This was plainly the hiding place of the auto thieves, and although none of the stolen cars were in evidence, the big packing boxes spoke for themselves.

"We'll see what's farther on," Frank decided.

He went ahead. Joe tiptoed close behind. The flashlight illuminated the rocky floor of the tunnel.

It began to widen out. Stacked against the wall they came upon more packing boxes, some of which had been torn open.

"More loot," Joe commented, in a whisper.

Every few steps, Frank halted and switched out the light. Then they stood in the darkness, listening. They had no desire to stumble on the auto thieves or reveal their own presence.

However, the boys heard not a sound. There was not a glimmer of light in the impenetrable gloom that lay before them.

A few yards farther, the tunnel widened out into a veritable cave. Here, as Frank turned the flashlight to and fro, and boys were confronted by a sight that made them gasp for the moment.

In the great rocky chamber, they saw three large pleasure cars and a small truck, parked close by the clammy walls.

"The stolen autos!" breathed Joe.

There stood four of the missing cars, undamaged, in this secret cavern in the bluffs. They had been driven in along the tunnel from the beach. It was an ideal hiding place and as the entrance to the tunnel was doubtless well masked, the cars were as safe from discovery as though they had been driven into the ocean. At least, so the thieves probably thought.

"We've found them!" Frank exclaimed.

All the missing cars were not hidden here, but the boys judged that the rest were probably stored farther on. For the flashlight revealed a dark opening in the rock at the other end of the cavern, an opening to a tunnel that no doubt led to other caves farther on.

The Hardy boys knew that the Shore Road bluffs, in certain places, contained caves and passages, some of which had never been entered. Although like most Bayport boys, they had done a certain amount of exploring along the beach, they had never heard of the existence of this under-ground labyrinth. It seemed strange to them that so elaborate a series of caves had never been explored and their existence was comparatively unknown.

"Wait until Bayport hears of this!" Joe said. "Let's get out of here and hurry back to town."

"I suppose we should," Frank admitted. "I'd like to know where those men went."

"If we go any farther they may catch us, and then we'd be out of luck."

"But if we start back to town we'll have to walk, and they might all clear out in the meantime. It would be a few hours before we could get back here with the police."

"We'd have the satisfaction of recovering the cars, anyway," Joe pointed out. "I believe in playing safe."

"I'd like the satisfaction of rounding up this gang as well."

Frank advanced toward the opening at the far side of the cave.

"I think I'll just poke along in here a little way and see where it leads," he said.

Joe was dubious. He was of a more cautious nature than his brother, and was satisfied to let well enough alone. They had found the missing cars. This alone was sufficient, he reasoned. Having come this far without mishap he did not like to risk spoiling their success. However, he followed Frank into the tunnel.

It was narrower than the one which had led them to the cave, and its sides were rocky and uneven, while the roof was low. It was quite evident that none of the cars could have been driven through this narrow space, and as the boys went on they found that the roof was lower and the walls even closer together.

Finally, the flashlight showed them that it was almost impossible to continue, as projecting rocks jutted out and there was just enough space to admit passage of one person. Beyond that, the tunnel seemed to close altogether.

"Guess this is a blind alley," said Frank. "We may as well turn back."

He handed the flashlight to Joe, who led the way on the return trip through the tunnel.

Suddenly there was an uproar immediately ahead, a clamorous, deafening crash. The boys jumped with astonishment. In the darkness of the subterranean cavern their nerves had been keyed up to a high pitch, and this tremendous clatter was so unexpected in the dead silence that had surrounded them that they were almost paralyzed with momentary fright.

There followed a rattling and bumping of rocks, and then silence once more.

"What was that?" exclaimed Joe, recovering from his scare.

"Sounded to me like a fall of rock." Frank's voice was shaky, for he had a suspicion of what had actually happened.

"It seemed mighty close."

"That's what I'm afraid of. It may have blocked up this tunnel."

Hastily, the boys went forward. In a few moments the flashlight revealed a sight at which their hearts sank.

The passage before them was completely closed up!

Great boulders, ledges of rock, and a heavy downpouring of earth formed an apparently impenetrable barrier ahead. A loose stone, no doubt dislodged when they went by a short time before, had given way and had brought down this miniature avalanche from the roof and sides of the tunnel.

"We're trapped!" Frank exclaimed.

CHAPTER XVIII

The Auto Thieves

The cave-in had imprisoned the Hardy boys.

The flashlight revealed not a single opening. The tunnel was blocked up, and for all the boys knew the barrier continued right to the outer cave.

"Now we're in for it," remarked Joe dubiously.

The boys realized that there was nothing to be gained by shouting for help. Even if their cries were heard, which would be unlikely with that solid mass of rock before them, it would only bring the auto thieves upon them.

"We'll have to work fast," said Frank. "There isn't any too much air in this place now, and if we don't get that rock cleared out of the way we'll be smothered."

"Do you mean to say we'll have to move all that rock aside?"

"What else is there to do?"

"It might take hours."

"That's better than dying in here," returned Frank philosophically. "You hold the light and I'll get busy."

He flung off his coat and attacked the formidable barrier.

Starting at the top, he moved rock after rock aside, placing them on the floor of the tunnel. The work was slow, and he seemed to make little progress. For, as the rocks were taken away, they showed only more rocks behind. It was evident that the cave-in had been of considerable extent.

Joe became impatient.

"I feel useless," he said. "You hold the light for a while and let me work."

"Put it in a ledge some place and we can both work."

Joe hunted around and managed to find a convenient ledge of rock on which to rest the flashlight. Its beam was directed at the barrier and, rid of the encumbrance, Joe was then able to lend a hand to the work of removing the debris.

Patiently, the brothers toiled, lifting aside the rocks and putting them back on the floor. Every little while a fresh shower of dirt and stones would come rattling down from the roof. The task seemed hopeless.

"Looks as if this goes on for yards," panted Joe wearily.

"We might get out in a couple of years." Frank said, resting for a moment. "Still, if we can only clear a small opening it'll be enough to let us out."

He attacked the barricade again with renewed vigor.

Wrenching at a large rock, he tugged and pulled until it became dislodged from the surrounding debris. Frank was just dragging the huge stone away when there came a warning rumble, a cry of alarm from Joe, and he leaped back.

He was just in time.

With a crash, a large section of the roof caved in, a flat ledge of rock just missing his head by inches. A mass of rubbish descended with a roar.

"Get out of the way!"

"Get out yourself!"

"Gee, it looks as if the whole roof might come down!"

"I got some dust in my eyes."

"Same here. Say, this is the worst yet."

"Humph! We'll be lucky if we are not buried alive."

Much crestfallen, the boys bumped into each other, rubbing their eyes and clearing their throats of the dry dust that had come down with the rocks.

Then they gazed at each other in dismay, and not without reason.

All the boys' work was undone. The barrier was now larger than it had ever been.

"That fixes it!" said Frank gloomily.

The ledge of rock that had given way was of such extent that it was impossible for any one to move it. Their path was completely blocked.

"No use working at *that* any more!"

Frank sat down on a rock, regarding the impassable heap.

"Buried alive," he remarked, at last.

"No one will ever find us here."

The boys realized the gravity of their plight. No one knew they were in the tunnel. No one had seen them enter. If they perished here, their bodies might never be recovered.

"Think we ought to start calling?" asked Joe hopefully.

"Looks as if we'll have to do something. Perhaps if we do call, the men won't hear us."

"How about going back along the tunnel? There was still a sort of opening, you remember."

"It's our only chance."

Frank had little hope that the tunnel had another outlet. However, he grabbed up the flashlight and the boys picked their way back along the rocky passage.

When they came to the place where the tunnel had seemed to end, they surveyed it dubiously.

"I'll go ahead," said Frank. "Like as not, I'll get stuck in here and you'll have to come in and pull me out."

He wedged himself into the opening between the rocks, holding the flashlight before him.

To his surprise he found that although there was a blank wall immediately ahead, the tunnel turned sharply to one side and in the glow of the light he saw that it continued for some little distance, a very narrow passage, but one that offered sufficient space for him to continue.

"It doesn't end here after all," he called back to Joe. "Perhaps it does lead outside."

He went on. Joe scrambled through the opening and followed close behind.

With growing elation Frank found that the tunnel continued. When he had gone about fifteen yards he rounded a sharp corner, and gave a cry of delight.

Here, on the wet floor, he spied the imprint of a man's shoe!

"There's been some one here before us," he said to Joe, in excitement. "A footprint!"

"Which way does it lead?"

"The way we're going. This isn't so hopeless after all."

This evidence that another human being had been in the tunnel gave the boys new courage.

"We'd better go quietly. Chances are that the auto thieves are somewhere around."

A few steps farther, and Frank spied a light in the distance. At first he thought it was only a reflection from his own flashlight, but when he switched it out, the light still glowed steadily through the darkness ahead.

They moved cautiously. Frank did not turn on the flashlight again. He was afraid it might be seen. Step by step, they moved forward, and the glow of the mysterious light became brighter. It was soon so strong that it even cast a certain amount of illumination into the tunnel and the boys saw that the passage was almost at an end.

Then they heard a voice.

They could not distinguish the words, but they could hear some one talking in a quick, rasping tone. Then another voice interrupted.

Frank laid a warning hand on his brother's sleeve.

"Quiet does it," he warned.

They crept forward.

The tunnel evidently opened into another cave. Edging ahead as close to the entrance of the passage as they dared, the boys saw that the light was from a huge lamp. It was not turned toward them, or the tunnel would have been bathed in a strong glare and they would have been seen, but it cast a strong radiance over a small cave in which half a dozen men were sitting.

The cavern was bare, but there were boxes scattered about on the rocky floor, and these provided makeshift seats. The lads caught only a glimpse of the eerie scene, the shadowy figures, and then they drew back, for two of the men were facing them and for a moment they thought the fellows could not have failed to see them. However, the glare of the immense lamp evidently blinded them to anything beyond, for they did not move.

A gruff voice spoke.

"Well, we can run that big touring car out to-night. Clancy says he can do the repainting to-morrow and we can get rid of it in a day or so if everything goes well."

"He took his time about selling that coupe."

"There was a hitch somewhere. He thought the dicks were watching his place, so he had to lay low for a few days."

"Well, I guess it's all right. I don't blame him for not taking any more chances than he has to."

"Rats!" said some one else. "He's takin' no chances! We've got away with everything fine so far and the cops haven't suspected any of us yet."

"Clancy's different," said the man with the gruff voice. "He's at the selling end, and that's where the danger lies. It's no trouble to steal these boats. The dicks don't try to trace 'em from that end, for they know there isn't much use. They watch until we try to get rid of 'em."

"Clancy's smart. He even burns out the engine numbers. When one of those cars leaves his hands, even the owner wouldn't recognize it if you took him for a ride in it."

"We've been making out all right so far, but we can't get too bold. The whole countryside is stirred up, and the farther we go the more chances we're taking."

"That's true. Just the same, we're about as safe here as any one can be. Nobody knows about these caves."

"Lucky break for us that they don't. If I didn't know about them I could walk up and down that beach for a month of Sundays and never spot an opening."

"That's a nice-lookin' roadster you landed to-night."

"It's been parked out on the Shore Road for two nights past. It seemed a shame to neglect a nice boat that way, so I took it in."

"What would anybody park a car out there for on a night like this? Wasn't there anybody around?"

"Not a soul. Mebbe the driver was out fishin' and got caught in the rain and didn't get back. Or he might have had engine trouble."

"It ran for you, didn't it?"

"Sure. But I can make 'em run when nobody else can."

"You sure know how to handle a car. I'll say that for you."

There was a stir in the cave.

"Here he comes now," announced some one.

Then the boys heard a familiar voice, a voice that sent a thrill of excitement through them.

"Coast is clear. You can run that car out now, Dan."

It was the voice of Gus Montrose!

CHAPTER XIX

Captured

Tensely, the Hardy boys crouched in the tunnel, as they heard the voice of the Dodds former hired man.

"It's a dirty night out," he was saying, "You're welcome to the trip, Dan."

"Still raining?"

"Pouring. I'm soaked to the skin," grumbled Montrose. "It's no fun, ploughing down through that gully."

"Well, you won't have much more to do to-night," said one of the men placatingly. "We landed a fine roadster while you were out."

"The one I was telling you about?"

"The same."

"Seems funny about that car being parked on the Shore Road three nights in a row. I saw it there the other evening and passed it up. Then last night I got in and would have driven it away, only I couldn't get it started. Different kind of car than any I've ever been in. I went out and found Sam and we were going back when we ran right into the car turning around in a lane."

"Didn't see who was in it, did you?"

"No. The headlights shone right in our eyes. Seemed like a couple of young fellows. If they had been a little slower we'd have had the car."

"Well, we have it now. They'll wish they wasn't so smart, leavin' it out in the rain that way."

"Nice wet walk they'll have if they live in Bayport," laughed Gus Montrose shortly. "I know who I *wish* owned it."

"Your little friends!"

"Those brats of Hardy boys," returned Gus. "Followed me for about three blocks to-day when I went uptown to meet Sam."

"What was the big idea?"

"Aw, they kid themselves that they're a couple of amateur detectives," rasped Montrose. "Just because they've been lucky in a couple of cases they think they gotta go spyin' on everybody."

"What made 'em spy on you?"

"How should I know? I guess Dodd must have put them up to it."

"They don't figger you're mixed up with these missin' cars, do they?"

"How could they? Nobody has anythin' on me," bragged Gus. "But I told them a few things, anyway. I told 'em to lay off followin' me or they'd get somethin' they wasn't lookin' for."

"What'd they say?"

"They backed down. Got scared and beat it."

"That's the way to talk to them," approved the man called Dan. "Scare the daylights out of them."

"Speakin' of daylight—it'll be daylight before you reach Atlantic City with that car if you don't hurry up."

"All right. All right. I'll start movin'," Dan growled.

"You might as well take some of that junk we got from the Importing Company's truck, and ask Clancy to sell it for us. And don't you forget to collect the money from him for the last car we turned over to him."

"I won't forget. Some of you guys had better come along and load a couple of those boxes for me."

There was a heavy tramping of feet, that indicated the men were leaving the cave. The Hardy boys could hear their receding footsteps and the diminishing voices. Finally the cave was in silence.

Frank peeped out of the tunnel.

"They've gone," he whispered.

"Are you going in?" questioned Joe.

"Sure. There's no one around."

He stepped out onto the rocky floor, with Joe at his heels.

The cave was not as large as the one in which the cars were stored, but from the boxes scattered around and from a litter of empty cigarette packages, burnt matches, old clothes, and other things lying about, it was clearly the meeting place of the gang.

"Well, we've found the auto thieves, all right. The next thing is to trap them."

"We can't do it alone, that's certain," said Joe. "I think we ought to get out of here as quickly as we can."

"There's probably only one opening to this place," answered Frank, flashing the light about the walls.

It fell on a dark opening through which the thieves had departed. There was no other passage apparent, beyond the one through which the boys had entered.

"Not much use going after them. They're probably all out in the cave where the cars are kept," remarked Joe.

"We'll just have to watch our chance."

"Let's take a look around here," remarked Frank, after a minute of silence.

"We'll have to be careful. They may come back and catch us," answered his brother.

"We'll watch out for that."

With caution the boys began to look around them.

"Look!" cried Frank in a low tone.

He bent down and from the rocky floor picked up a big bunch of keys.

"Auto keys," came from Joe.

"Yes, and all different. I suppose they have all the keys necessary to unlock any car."

"More than likely."

Near the keys they found a dark coat and a cap.

"I guess the keys dropped out of that coat," remarked Frank.

"Looks like it." Joe's gaze traveled to a spot back of the coat. "Look, a wig!" he exclaimed.

"That shows they go out disguised."

"It sure does. Say, we're getting to the bottom of this mystery!"

"I hope so."

The boys explored the under-ground chamber, but found nothing of further interest.

"So we were right, after all," Frank said. "Gus Montrose is mixed up with the auto thieves."

"He probably discovered these caves in the first place, and saw how they could be used for concealing stolen goods. Perhaps this place was used by smugglers long ago."

"Probably. They are natural caves, and it's easily seen that they've been used for a long time. Some of the tunnels look as if they'd been blasted out to widen them. We're certainly lucky to have found their hiding place, for we'd never have found it unless we'd been brought here."

"From their talk, they evidently drive the cars to Atlantic City from here."

"Must have a secret road of some kind, or they'd never get through."

"Montrose spoke of coming through a gully."

"There is a gully near the Dodd farm. Now that I come to think of it, I believe there is an abandoned road through it. The place has been overgrown with brush for the past five years, though."

"Perhaps they cleared it out."

"The road used to lead out to one of the private, right-of-way roads in the back township. Since the Shore Road was extended, it's never been used. I'll bet that's what they're doing—using that old road and bringing the cars out the back way. The police haven't been watching the private roads at all."

"It's a smart scheme. Well, it won't last much longer."

Suddenly, a voice rang out, clear and sharp:

"I'll get the lantern. It's right here."

Startled, the boys wheeled about. The voice seemed to be right beside them.

Instantly, they realized that it was only a trick of the echoes, and that the voice came from the passage leading into the cave.

Some one was approaching. They could hear his heavy boots clumping on the rocky floor.

"Quick! The tunnel!" whispered Frank.

He sped across the cave toward the opening in the wall. But they had moved farther away from their hiding place than they imagined. By the time the brothers reached the passage, they heard a cry of alarm behind them.

"Who's that?"

They scrambled into the tunnel.

Another shout, footsteps across the floor, and then the lantern cast its beam directly on the entrance of the passage. It was a powerful light and the boys knew they had been seen.

The man in the cave began shouting for help:

"Gus! Sam! Come here! Quick!"

His voice echoed from the walls.

The Hardy boys heard a faint shout from outside the cave.

"What's the matter?"

"Some one in here. Hurry up!"

The uproar out in the cave grew in volume as other members of the gang joined their comrade. There was a hasty gabble of voices.

"There was some one in the cave when I came back for the light," shouted the man who had discovered the boys. "They beat it into that tunnel. I just saw them."

"Sam, go around and watch the other side!" ordered some one sharply. "That tunnel goes out into the big cave."

The thieves were evidently unaware of the cave-in that had blocked the passage.

Frank and Joe retreated beyond the first bend. They were trapped. The barricade cut off their flight, and they knew they were facing certain capture.

"The guns!" snapped Frank.

He drew his revolver from his pocket and fired into the darkness, around the corner.

There was a shout of alarm.

"Get back! Get back, Gus! They've got guns!"

Then followed a wild scrambling, as the man who had pursued them into the tunnel hustled back to safety.

Frank pressed himself against the rocky wall, in case any of the gang should enter and open fire on them. But the thieves had been frightened by his shot.

"That'll hold them for a while!"

"How long?" Joe reminded him. "They have us trapped, Frank. We can't go back. They'll starve us out."

"We won't give up without a fight."

There was a tremendous uproar out in the cave. The men were talking loudly and their voices were intensified by the tumultuous echoes of the place.

"Follow them in!" some one shouted. But Gus snarled:

"We can't. They're armed."

"Well," said Frank quietly, "we have enough bullets to keep them back for a while, at any rate."

"They'll get us, in the long run."

"I suppose so."

Then the Hardy boys heard the voice of the man called Sam. He came into the cave, shouting:

"They can't get out! There's been a cave-in and the tunnel is jammed up with rock."

"Good!" exclaimed Gus exultantly. "Here! Hand me that light."

There was a moment of silence. Then the powerful lantern was evidently turned toward the mouth of the tunnel, for the light gleamed on the walls. As they were just around the bend in the passage, the boys could not be seen, but the glaring light was reflected from the rocks.

"They're out of sight," muttered some one. "Try a shot!"

Instantly, there was an explosion, as a revolver roared. The echoes were deafening in that confined space.

Something whizzed past Frank's head and smacked against the rock.

The bullet, aimed for the rock wall, had ricocheted across the bend and had missed him by a hairbreadth.

This was too close for comfort. The revolver crashed again, and there was a cry from Joe.

"Are you hurt?" asked Frank anxiously.

"No. But the bullet glanced off the rocks. I think it went through my sleeve. It sure was close."

Their voices had been heard by the men in the cave.

"That's got 'em scared!" yelled Gus.

The boys retreated out of range of the glancing bullets.

"We're up against it," Frank admitted. "If we stay here they'll starve us out. If we try to rush them, we'll get shot."

"I guess we'll have to surrender."

"Looks as if there's nothing else for it. We'll give ourselves up and take our chances on escape. The way things are, we're liable to be shot."

He edged back toward the bend in the passage. There was a lull in the firing.

"We give up!" he shouted.

A yell of triumph followed.

"Now you're talkin' sense!" shouted Gus. "Throw your gun out here."

Frank hurled his revolver around the corner and it clattered on the rocks. Some one crawled into the passage and retrieved it.

"Now come out with your hands up."

Bitter though their defeat was, the Hardy boys had to acknowledge that the odds were against them. With their arms in the air, they came around the corner, into the glare of the big lamp. Step by step, they advanced until, at the junction of cave and tunnel, they were seized by their captors.

CHAPTER XX

Tables Turned

The dazzling glare of the big lamp was turned full in the faces of the Hardy boys. They heard a gasp of astonishment.

"Why, it's a couple of kids!" exclaimed one of the men.

"Couple of kids!" rasped Gus Montrose, in astonishment. "Do you know who we've got here?"

"Who?"

"Them Hardy boys. The pair that followed me yesterday."

"What?"

"It's them. The very same spyin' pair of brats." A rough hand seized Frank's shoulder and swung him around. "I'd know them anywhere. Fenton Hardy's kids."

The name of Fenton Hardy made a distinct impression on the gang. There were mutterings of anger and fear.

"The detective's boys, eh?" growled one. "What are you doin' here, boys?"

"That's for you to find out," replied Frank shortly.

"Is that so? Well, you've got no business here. You know that, don't you?"

"Your own business here doesn't seem any too lawful."

"Never mind about us. You come spyin' around here and you've got to expect to take the consequences. What'll we do with 'em, Gus?"

"They're not goin' out of here, that's certain. We're not goin' to let them go back home and tell what they've seen."

"Or what they heard. How long were you two boys hidin' in that tunnel?"

"You can try to find that out, too," retorted Frank.

"Smart, ain't you?" snarled Montrose. "You won't be so smart when we get through with you. Anybody got a rope?"

"Here's some," said a man in the background.

"Give it here, then. We'll tie these brats up and keep 'em until we figure out what to do with 'em."

"You let us alone," said Frank.

"You have no right to make us prisoners," added Joe.

"We'll take the right."

"You are mighty high-handed."

"Rats! You'll be lucky if you don't get worse," growled one of the auto thieves.

"We ought to throw 'em into the bay," added another.

"Yes, with a few big stones in each pocket to hold 'em down," came the response from a third.

"Shut up, you all talk too much," commanded Montrose. "Where is that rope you spoke of?"

He snatched a length of heavy cord from the man who handed it to him. Frank was turned roughly around and his arms thrust behind his back. In a moment his wrists were firmly tied. Joe received the same treatment. The boys were bound and helpless.

"Put 'em over in the corner," ordered Montrose.

The boys were pushed and jostled across the rocky floor and were made to sit down against the wall at the back of the cave. The big lamp was turned on them all this time and they could set the faces of none of their captors.

"This is a fine mess!" grumbled one of the men. "It ruins the whole game."

Montrose turned on him.

"We were going to clear out to-morrow anyway, weren't we?" he said. "We'll just have to work a little quicker, that's all. Instead of sending one car out to-night and the rest to-morrow night, we'll get busy and drive 'em all out right now."

"What about these kids?"

"Leave 'em here."

"They'll starve," said one man dubiously.

"What of that?" demanded Gus Montrose. "They'd have had us all landed in jail if they could."

"Well—I don't hold—"

"They brought it on themselves. Who'll ever find 'em here, anyway?"

"I'd rather take 'em out to the railway and dump 'em into an empty box car. They might be five hundred miles away before anybody found 'em. That would give us plenty of time to scatter."

Murmurs of approval from the other men greeted this plan.

"Do as you like," growled Montrose. "I figger we ought to clear out and leave 'em here."

Suddenly the big lamp, which one of the gang was holding, dimmed and went out.

"What's the matter now? Turn on that light, Joe."

"It's gone out."

"D'you think we're blind? Of course it's out. Turn it on."

"The lamp's gone dead, I think. There's somethin' wrong with it. It won't light again." They could hear the man tinkering at the lamp. "No use," he said at last.

The cave was in pitch blackness. One of the men struck a match, and it cast a faint illumination.

"There's candles around here somewhere, ain't there?" asked Gus Montrose.

"Whole box of 'em around if I can find them."

The man with the match moved off into another part of the cave. He fumbled around for a while, then announced with a grunt of satisfaction:

"Here they are." He lit one of the candles, brought it over and stood it on a box.

"Light some more," ordered Gus.

The man did as he was told. In a few moments half a dozen candles provided a fair amount of light in the gloom of the cave.

"That's better."

Just then there was a shout from the passage leading into the main cave. Gus Montrose wheeled about.

"Who's that?"

The men crouched tensely.

"I don't know," whispered one. "We're all here but Dan."

In a moment footsteps could be heard in the passage. Then a voice:

"Hey—come out and help me. My car got stuck!"

"It's Dan," said Montrose, in a tone of relief.

A man entered the cave. He stopped short, in surprise.

"For the love of Pete!" he exclaimed. "What's this? Prayer meetin'?"

"The lamp went out," explained Gus. "We caught a couple of kids spyin' on us."

The newcomer whistled.

"Spies, eh? Where are they?"

"We got 'em tied up. In the corner, there."

Dan, who was evidently the man who had driven the roadster down from the Shore Road, came over and regarded the Hardy boys.

"This don't look so good," he said. "What are we goin' to do?"

"We'll attend to 'em," growled Montrose. "Your job is to drive that car in to Clancy's place. The rest of us are bringin' the other cars in to-night."

"Clearin' out a day earlier, eh?"

"That's the idea."

"Well, you'll have to come out and help me get my car out of the mud or none of us will get away."

"You're bogged?"

"Up to the hubs. There's been so much rain that the gully road is now knee-deep in mud."

"All right. We'll come and get you out. How many men do you want?"

"It'll take the whole crowd of us."

"No, it won't. We're not goin' to leave these kids here alone. Joe, here, can stay and watch 'em."

"They're tied, ain't they?"

"What of it? I'm not trustin' to no ropes. Somebody's got to stay and keep an eye on them."

"I'll stay," grumbled the man addressed as Joe.

"I don't care who stays," snapped Dan. "If you don't come out and help drag that car out of the mud it'll be in so deep we'll never get it out. Come on."

The men trooped out of the cave. Joe, who was left behind, sat down on a box and regarded the lads balefully. However, he said nothing. Gus came back through the passage.

"You might as well be loadin' some of those boxes into the other cars, while we're away," he said. "Take a look in every little while and see that those kids are still tied up."

The man grumbled assent, and followed Gus back down the passage.

The Hardy boys were left alone in the light of the flickering candles ranged about the gloomy cave.

"Well, we've lost out, I guess," remarked Frank bitterly. "If we ever do get back to Bayport it won't be until the auto thieves have all cleared out of here with the cars."

"It doesn't look very bright," sighed Joe.

Suddenly, Frank sat up.

"Say!" he exclaimed. "Did they take your revolver?"

"No. I guess they didn't know I had one."

"They took mine and missed yours. You still have it?"

"Right in my pocket."

"Good!"

"What good is it when I can't get at it?"

"If you can, we have only this chap Joe to deal with." The flame of the candle caught Frank's eye. He had an inspiration. "If only I could just get these ropes off my wrists!" he said.

Frank edged over toward the candle. Then, with his back to the flame, he lowered his arms until the cord that bound his wrists was within an inch of the wick.

A candle does not throw out much heat, but that little flame seared Frank's wrists and he had to clench his teeth to keep from crying out with the pain.

He could hold the rope in the flame for a few moments only, and then he withdrew it. When the scorching pain had somewhat subsided, he tried again. The flame licked at the heavy cord, weakening it strand by strand.

"Look out, Frank," warned Joe.

Frank scrambled back to the corner.

He was just in time. Heavy footsteps in the passage announced the approach of their guard, who came to the entrance, looked at them sullenly for a moment, then turned away again. He went back to the outer cave.

Hardly had he disappeared when Frank was back at the candle. He thrust the rope into the flame again.

When he could stand the burning heat no longer he withdrew and tried to break his bonds by sheer force. But, although the ropes had been weakened, they refused to break. He returned to the flame again, and on the next attempt he was successful. So many strands had been burned through that the cords snapped, and his hands were free.

Quickly, Frank went over to his brother. First of all, he took the revolver from Joe's pocket and put it on the rock beside him, in readiness. Then he knelt down and tugged at the strong ropes that bound Joe's wrists so tightly.

The knots were stubborn, but he finally undid them. The ropes fell apart and Joe was free.

"Now!" gritted Frank, picking up the revolver. "We'll go and attend to our friend in the cave."

"Hadn't we better wait here for him? There may be some one with him."

"I guess you're right. We'll take him by surprise the next time he comes back."

Frank went over to the side of the tunnel that led out into the main cave.

"Bring those ropes with you, Joe. Take the other side."

Joe picked up the cords that had bound his own wrists, and took up his position at the other side of the entrance. There the boys waited.

In a short time they heard heavy footsteps in the tunnel. Their guard was returning. Frank gripped the revolver. The lads pressed themselves against the wall. The footsteps drew closer. Then a dark figure emerged from the opening.

Frank stepped swiftly out behind the rascal and pressed the revolver against his back.

"Hands up!" he ordered sharply.

Their victim gave a cry of fright. He had been startled almost out of his wits. His hands shot up.

"Stand where you are!"

Frank still pressed the muzzle of the revolver against their erstwhile captor while Joe searched the man for weapons and found a small automatic in the fellow's hip pocket. This he took.

"Put your hands behind your back!" ordered Frank.

Their prisoner obeyed.

Quickly, Joe tied the man's wrists.

"Go over and sit on that box!"

Muttering and grumbling with rage, the fellow did so. Joe hunted around until he found another length of rope, and with this he bound the man's feet.

"I guess you'll be all right here until the others come back," Frank told the captive.

"If ever I get free of these ropes—"

"Keep quiet," ordered Frank, brandishing the revolver menacingly. Their prisoner was silenced abruptly.

"Blow out the candles, Joe. He might think of the same idea."

The candles were blown out. The boys were in complete darkness.

"Hey!" roared their prisoner. "You're not goin' to leave me here alone in the dark, are you?"

"Exactly. Where's our flashlight, Joe?"

"I have it here. It was in my pocket." Joe turned on the light. In its glow they saw their prisoner, bound hand and foot, sitting disconsolately on the box.

"Fine. We'll go now."

They left the cave, unmindful of the appeals of the auto thief, and made their way down a passage that led into the outer cavern where the stolen cars were stored. The light showed them a large opening that they had not seen when they were in the place on the first occasion.

"I guess this is the way they drive the cars out," remarked Frank. "We'll go out the way we came in. We won't be so likely to meet the others."

The boys hastened down the far passage. They hurried past their roadster, on through the tunnel. At last they saw a gleam of light ahead, shining faintly in the distance.

CHAPTER XXI

At the Farmhouse

In a few moments, the Hardy boys had emerged from the passage and stood in a heavy clump of bushes that obscured the entrance to the tunnel in the bluff. Brushing aside the trees, they stepped out onto the beach.

The light they had seen was from a ship, steaming into Bayport Harbor, and in the distance they could see a dim yellow haze—the lights of the city.

Above them towered the rocky bluff. Farther down the beach they saw the break in the cliffs where the gully ran back toward the Shore Road.

"We can't go that way," Frank decided quickly. "The thieves are up in the gully helping get that car out of the mud."

Joe looked up at the steep cliff.

"We certainly can't climb up here."

"We can go out the way we came in. The roadster came down the beach, you remember. We may find the trail back."

The storm had spent its force and a fine drizzle of rain was now falling. The boys went back down the beach, the flashlight illuminating the way.

By the smoothness of the beach they knew that this was the route the car had followed on the way in. Later on they came to an open stretch of sand. Beyond that lay rocks.

There was a break in the cliff, and by the flashlight, the boys picked out an automobile track in a patch of sand, leading toward low bushes that masked the entrance to a gully.

"This is the place we're looking for," said Frank. "I'll bet the roadster came down through here."

He pushed aside the wet bushes. In the damp grass, the track was still plainly visible.

The gully was dank with undergrowth, but there were evidences of a wide trail.

"We're getting there, anyway. From the direction, this ought to take us up to the Shore Road."

"What shall we do then?" asked Joe. "Walk to Bayport?"

"We shouldn't have to. There are farms along the road. We ought to be able to telephone to town."

"To the police?"

"Sure! Police and state troopers. We can't round up this gang by ourselves, and we haven't any too much time to get help, as it is."

"Well, we at least know where they can trace the stolen cars. That's one consolation."

"You mean Clancy?"

"In Atlantic City. The police ought to be able to catch him without any trouble."

The boys struggled on up the gully, along the trail that led through the wet woods toward the Shore Road. The underbrush had been cleared away for the passage of the stolen cars, and they found no difficulty following this strange road.

Finally, Frank gave a cry of delight.

"We're at the road!"

He emerged from the bushes, raced across a grassy stretch, and scrambled up onto the highway. It was, indeed, the Shore Road at last.

The boys looked about them. Some distance away they saw a gleam of light.

"A farmhouse! We'll try it."

They hurried down the road, and at length the flashlight revealed the entrance to a lane. Splashing through the water-filled ruts, the boys made their way between the crooked fences toward the dim mass of farm buildings.

"This place seems sort of familiar," remarked Joe.

"I was thinking the same thing."

"I know now! It's the Dodd farm!"

Joe was right. When the boys entered the barnyard, in spite of the fact that darkness obscured their surroundings, they knew from the size and position of the buildings that they had reached the Dodd place.

"This makes it easier. They have a telephone," said Frank.

"And that light in the window shows that some one is up."

They hurried to the door of the farmhouse and knocked. In a little while the door was flung open and Jack Dodd confronted them.

"Who's there?" he asked, peering out into the darkness. Then he exclaimed with astonishment: "The Hardy boys! What on earth are you doing here at this hour? Come in!"

Frank and Joe entered. They were wet and bedraggled, and Jack Dodd looked at them curiously.

"I was working late at my studies," he explained. "What happened? Did your car get stalled?"

"We've found the auto thieves—and the stolen cars!" Frank told him quickly.

"They're not far from here, either. We want to use your telephone," added Joe.

"The auto thieves!" gasped Jack incredulously. "You've found them?"

"The whole gang. And if we move fast we'll be able to land the outfit," answered Frank.

Jack quickly realized the situation. There was no time to be lost. He led the way into a hallway and pointed to the telephone.

"There you are!"

As it was a rural telephone line, he had to explain to the Hardy boys the proper number of rings necessary to arouse Central.

It took Frank some little time to get Central, as calls at that hour were infrequent out the Shore Road. The boys waited impatiently, but at last a sleepy voice answered the ring, and Frank hurriedly demanded the Bayport police headquarters.

He was soon in touch with the desk sergeant. He outlined the situation quickly.

"The gang were all up in the gully hauling a car out of the mud when we left. They'll be clearing out as soon as they discover their man in the cave, so you'll have to hurry," said Frank.

"I'll put every man available on it right away," the sergeant promised. "I'll call up Chief Collig at his house and tell him, too."

"Fine! Will you notify the state troopers? It's outside the city limits, you know."

"I'll call them up."

"You'll need a strong force of men, for this crowd are armed, and they'll have a hundred hiding places in the woods and along that beach. We'll keep a watch on the gully roads until you get here, and we'll wait for you."

"Good work! Are you sure it's the gang we've been after?"

"Certain. We found most of the stolen cars."

The sergeant was astonished.

"Found 'em? Where?"

"We'll tell you all about it later. In the meantime, get as many men out here as you can."

The sergeant disconnected abruptly. Frank had a mental picture of the activity that would follow in Bayport police circles on receipt of the news.

Jack Dodd was eagerly waiting for information.

"You mean to say you've actually found the thieves!" he exclaimed joyfully. "Then that means Dad and I will be cleared!"

"I hope so," Frank told his chum.

Briefly, the Hardy lads explained how they had hidden in the locker of the roadster, how the car had been driven away by one of the thieves, how they had overheard the conversation of the gang in the cave, how they had been captured and how they had escaped.

The Dodd household had been aroused, and Mr. Dodd came hurrying downstairs, half dressed. When he learned what had happened he hustled into the rest of his clothes and produced an ancient rifle from the back shed.

"I want to be in on this," he said grimly. "Those thieves have caused us more trouble than enough, and I'd like to get some of my own back."

Jack snatched up a flashlight.

"We'd better go out and watch the gully roads," Frank said.

"I know the road they drive out!" exclaimed Jack. "It's just a little below the end of our lane. There's an abandoned road that used to lead back to that old right-of-way, but I don't see how they reach it, for there's a fence to cross."

"Probably they take down the bars and drive through the field," said Mr. Dodd. "Now that you mention it, I always did think part of that fence looked pretty rickety."

They left the house and hurried down the lane toward the main road.

"We'd better split up," Frank suggested. "I have a revolver—it's Joe's, by the way—and Mr. Dodd has a rifle. Jack has a flashlight and so has Joe. Two of us can watch the first gully."

"You and Joe know the place where you came out onto the Shore Road," said Jack. "You'd better watch there. Dad and I will take the upper gully."

"Good! We'll just keep watch until the police arrive."

They separated at the end of the lane. Frank and Joe hurried off down the road, while the Dodds went in the opposite direction. When the boys reached the gully that led down to the beach they settled down to wait.

Because they were impatient and because they realized that the gang would doubtless scatter to points of safety as soon as their escape was discovered, it seemed to them that the police were a long time in coming. In reality it was not long, because the desk sergeant had lost no time in sending out the alarm.

The roar of approaching motorcycles and the drone of a speeding motor car were the first intimations of the arrival of the police and the state troopers. Even before the machines came into view their clamor could be heard.

Then dazzling headlights flashed over the rise. Frank ran out into the road, waving the flashlight, and in a few moments the first motorcycle skidded to a stop.

"Where are they?" shouted a trooper.

"There are two ways in. We have two men watching the other gully. If you'll put some of your men up there on guard, we can take you down to the beach from here."

The other motorcycles came up, and finally an automobile which was crowded with police officers. Everybody talked at once. The first trooper, however, quickly took charge of the impending raid, and in decisive tones he gave his orders.

"Johnson, take three policemen and go on up to the other gully. These lads say you'll find a farmer and his son on guard. They have a flashlight, so you can't miss them. Watch that gully and grab any one who comes out."

One of the troopers got back onto his motorcycle. All but three of the policemen scrambled out of their car. The motorcycle leaped forward with a roar, and the automobile followed close behind.

"All right," said the trooper. "We'll leave one man here to watch the road in case any of them slip through our fingers. The rest of us will go on down this gully."

"Callahan, stay on duty here," ordered the sergeant in charge of the police officers. Callahan, a burly policeman, saluted. His face, revealed for a moment in the glare of a flashlight, showed that he did not relish the assignment, evidently preferring to go where there was promise of some excitement.

"All right, boys. Lead the way!"

Frank and Joe went across the grass beside the road and plunged into the undergrowth at the entrance of the gully. Their hearts were pounding with excitement. The moment of success was at hand.

Behind them trooped nine stalwart officers, heavily armed.

Down the sloping gully they went. The trooper in charge fell in step beside Frank and the boy explained the situation that lay ahead.

"Two openings to the caves, eh?" said the trooper. "Well, we have them cornered. That is, if the birds haven't flown."

They came to the beach. Their boots clattered on the rocks as the men hurried forward.

At length the bushes that concealed the entrance to the first tunnel were in sight.

CHAPTER XXII

The Round-Up

"This is the place!" Frank Hardy excitedly told the officer in charge of the party. "The tunnel is right behind those bushes."

"Mighty well hidden," the trooper commented. "Do you think you can find the other opening?"

"It's farther down the beach."

"I think I could find it," volunteered Joe.

"Take three of these men and watch that part of the beach, at any rate." The trooper detailed three men to accompany Joe. "I'll wait until I see your flashlight signal," he said. "When you find the place where they drive the cars out, turn the light on and off. Then wait for my whistle."

Joe and the men with him hurried on down the beach. The others waited in silence near the entrance to the tunnel.

Eventually they saw the blinking light that plainly told them that the outer passage was guarded.

"Fine," said the trooper. He raised the whistle to his lips. "All ready, men?"

"All set," answered one of the constables, in a low voice.

The shrill blast of the whistle sounded through the night. With one accord, the men leaped forward, plunged into the bushes, and crowded into the tunnel. Their flashlights made the dark passage as bright as day.

As they entered they could hear a confused uproar ahead. The roar of an automobile, the sound magnified tenfold in the subterranean passages, crashed out. There were shouts, cries of warning and alarm.

"We've got them trapped!" shouted the trooper.

They stumbled down the rocky passage. A man came blundering around a corner, right into the arms of the foremost officer. He was seized, there was a gleam of metal, a click, and the auto thief was handcuffed before he fully realized what had happened.

"One!" counted the sergeant. "Now for the others!"

They passed the Hardy boys' roadster and caught a glimpse of a man fleeing before them into the main cave. The trooper drew his revolver and sent a shot over the fellow's head.

The man came to an abrupt stop and raised his arms. He surrendered without a fight.

"Two!" yelled the sergeant gleefully, pouncing on his prisoner. Another pair of handcuffs was produced, the chain was slipped through the chain of the other thief's shackles, and the pair were swiftly manacled together.

The officers plunged on into the main cave.

In the glare of the flashlights they saw the truck and one of the pleasure cars standing by the wall. The two other cars that had been in the cave had disappeared. No men were in sight.

The raiding party heard the roar of a racing engine, a grinding of brakes, and a confusion of shouts.

"They're getting out!" Frank Hardy shouted. He pointed to the huge opening in the wall, through which the car had disappeared.

With the police at his heels, he headed down the passage. It was wider than the one through which they had entered, and the rocky floor gave way to earth, in which ruts were clearly visible.

Ahead of them they heard a shot, then more yells.

"Joe and his men are on the job," Frank reflected.

He was right. They reached the mouth of the passage, and there they came upon a large touring car. Two men were standing up in the front seat, arms upraised, and in the glare of the headlights they could see Joe and the three officers pointing their weapons at the pair.

The round-up was soon over. One of the policemen scrambled into the automobile and clapped handcuffs on the two men. The trooper, standing on the running board, turned a flashlight upon them.

The surly features of Gus Montrose were revealed. The other man was his companion, Sam.

"All out!" snapped the officer, urging the crestfallen thieves out of the car.

They stepped out sullenly.

"Well, here's four of 'em, anyway!" declared the trooper. He turned to Frank. "Do you think there are any more?"

"There's still another. He was the chap who got stuck in the mud up in the gully. Perhaps he's up there yet, if the Dodds haven't caught him on the way out."

The trooper despatched two of his men up the gully road at once, to see if they could locate the other member of the gang.

"Well, Montrose," he said, turning to the former hired man, "so we've landed you at last."

Gus looked down at the handcuffs.

"I'd have been clear away if it wasn't for them brats of boys!" he said viciously.

"They were a little too smart for you and your gang."

The four auto thieves were herded together and an officer with drawn revolver was put on guard.

"I guess we'll go back into the cave and see what we can find," decided the trooper. Leaving the prisoners under guard, he and some of his men, together with the Hardy boys, went back into the main cavern, where the officers inspected the remaining cars and the loot that they found stored there. The sergeant rubbed his hands gleefully.

"Everything's here," he said. "At least, everything we need to make an airtight case against that gang. And we'll recover the rest of the stuff without much trouble, I imagine."

He turned to Joe Hardy.

"You said you learned where they were sending the cars?" he inquired.

"They spoke of a man named Clancy in Atlantic City. They drove the stolen cars out through the gully, across the Shore Road onto one of those old private roads, and then down the coast."

"That's all we want to know. We'll wire the Atlantic City police as soon as we get back to headquarters."

"We might as well bring back as much of this stuff as we can," said the trooper. "Make a triumphal procession of it."

Some of the loot they found already loaded into the small truck, in preparation for the get-away, and in a short time they had cleared the cave and the passage of the other packing boxes. One of the officers was assigned to the wheel of the truck and another was detailed to drive the other car. Frank and Joe announced their intention of driving their own roadster back to Bayport.

Before long, the little cavalcade was in readiness to start.

In the lead was the touring car, with four sullen and defeated auto thieves huddled in the back seat, a trooper and a constable in front.

Next came the truck, loaded with stolen goods. It was followed by the other pleasure car, with the sergeant and the other officers sitting at their ease. Behind it came the roadster, with the Hardy boys.

The foremost car followed the gully road without difficulty. The headlights illuminated the way clearly, and the automobiles lumbered up toward the Shore Road. They had no trouble in the muddy section where Dan had come to grief, for the thieves had covered the spot with branches and the cars crossed without becoming stalled.

The road led through the woods and finally ended in a seemingly impenetrable screen of trees.

Gus Montrose jeered.

"Try and get through there!" he said.

Puzzled, the driver got out and advanced toward the heavy thickets. It seemed impossible to go any farther, and yet the tire marks of other cars were visible right up to the undergrowth. He gave one of the trees a kick, and it fell back. The secret was revealed. A cunningly contrived platform held the trees in place, and it swung back, in the manner of a gate. When a car passed through, it was drawn shut again and gave the appearance of an unbroken mass of foliage.

This explained why the secret road had never been discovered and why the thieves were able to drive their cars out through the gully without great risk of detection. The loose trees formed a perfect screen.

At last the Shore Road was in sight. The foremost car lumbered up onto the highway. In its headlights a strange group stood revealed.

There, in front of a fine sedan, stood Mr. Dodd, rifle in hand, confronting the remaining auto thief. With him were Jack Dodd and the officer who had been despatched to their assistance.

The thief, presumably the man called Dan, was sitting disconsolately on the bumper of the car, handcuffs about his wrists.

"We got him!" shouted Jack, in excitement, as the cars lumbered out of the bush. "Held him up just as he came out onto the road."

"Fine work!" applauded the sergeant, scrambling out. "This just about cleans up the gang—all except Clancy."

Dan looked up sharply.

"How do you know about Clancy?"

"Never mind. We know all about him. And he'll be behind the bars with the rest of you before long, if I'm not mistaken."

The trooper who had been in charge of the round-up came up at this juncture.

"Another, eh?" he said cheerfully. "Well, the little procession is growing. Better join the parade, boys."

He assigned one of the men to replace Dan at the wheel of the stolen car.

"We'll let you be a passenger, for a change," he said, motioning the thief to the back seat. "Guest of honor."

From Dan's expression, as he took his seat, he did not appreciate the compliment.

"You'd better come to town with us for the finish," called Frank to the Dodds.

"I wouldn't miss it for a farm," Jack said, as he scrambled into the roadster with them.

So, with police, auto thieves, troopers, the Dodds and the Hardy boys duly seated in the various cars, the procession started for Bayport. One of the officers drove back the police car, with the motorcycles securely lashed in place on the running boards, and one piled in the back seat.

In the Hardy boys' roadster, jubilation prevailed. Jack Dodd was loud in his praises of the work the lads had done, and beneath it all was the undercurrent of intense relief because he knew the capture of the gang would clear himself and his father from suspicion.

"That's the best part of it, for us," said Joe Hardy, when their chum mentioned this.

CHAPTER XXIII

The Mystery Solved

The capture and subsequent trial of the automobile thieves provided Bayport with one of its biggest sensations in many a day. Although some of the gang stubbornly insisted on their innocence, the evidence against them was so complete that the state had no trouble in securing prosecutions against them all, and they were sentenced to long terms of imprisonment in the state penitentiary.

The man, Clancy, was arrested in Atlantic City and was convicted with the rest of the gang, on charges of receiving and disposing of stolen property. The Bayport police notified Atlantic City detectives, and Clancy's arrest was accomplished within an hour after the other members of the gang were lodged in the cells.

Gus Montrose was questioned by detectives shortly after the triumphant procession reached the city. This was done at the request of Mr. Dodd, who was anxious that he and Jack should be cleared of all suspicion in connection with the thefts as quickly as possible.

Montrose saw that the game was up. He admitted that his former employer knew nothing of the stolen cars.

"It was while I was working for Mr. Dodd that I found the caves in the bluffs," he confessed. "I used to go down to the beach a lot to fish, and one day I found the opening into the tunnel and explored the big cave. I thought at the time that it would be a good place to hide stolen goods. Then one day I met Sam. He had just been released from the pen and we got to talking together and he said he thought there would be good money to be picked up stealin' cars."

"Where did you pick up the rest of the crowd?"

"Sam's friends, mostly. When I told Sam about the caves in the bluffs, he said it was just what we needed and he asked me if there was any roads in. I said there wasn't, but we could make roads in and out through the gullies, and cover 'em up. Then I told him about the old private road through to the back townships. He come with me and we looked the place over and he said it was just right. He wrote to some of his friends and they come on here and we started to work."

"That was when you quit your job at the Dodd place?"

"I didn't want to quit, for I figgered people wouldn't be so likely to think I was mixed up with the car stealin' if I kept on workin', but it took up so much of my time that Mr. Dodd let me go."

"Who did the actual car stealing?"

"The rest of the fellows. My job was to keep my eyes open for good chances. People would see me goin' along the Shore Road and think nothin' of it, but if any of the other boys went out, somebody might see 'em and think it queer, because they was strangers. Mostly I stayed down on the beach fishin', and kept watchin' the road for places people parked their cars. Then I'd signal to Dan or one of the others and they'd come and drive the car away."

"Fishing!" exclaimed Jack Dodd. "I'll bet that's how my rod disappeared."

"I took it, after your father fired me," Montrose admitted.

"How did it come to get into the car found behind Dodd's barn?" one of the detectives demanded.

"That was a car Dan had stolen; but the owner chased him in another car and he couldn't get down the gully without bein' seen. Dan had picked me up and I had the rod with me. He drove the car up behind the barn and hid it there and we got back to the cave on foot. I left the rod in the car."

"Well, that explains everything," the detective remarked. He turned to Mr. Dodd. "There shouldn't be any difficulty withdrawing the charges against you and your son."

"It takes a big load off my mind," declared the farmer. "It was a terrible worry to have that hangin' over our heads when we knew we were innocent."

"You must admit that the circumstances looked bad. We only did what we thought was our duty."

"I suppose so. Well, if the charges are withdrawn we won't say anything more about it."

Withdrawal of the charges was a formality that was soon executed.

In the week following, both Mr. Dodd and Jack were congratulated by scores of people on having been cleared of all suspicion in connection with the Shore Road mystery. The bail money was returned to Mr. Hardy and the boys.

Frank and Joe Hardy were the real heroes of the case. Their good work in discovering the hiding place of the auto thieves and in notifying the police in time to capture the gang, earned them praise from all quarters. The Bayport newspaper gave much space to the affair and the story of the lads' adventures in the cave provided thrilling reading.

"Some detectives, Frank and Joe!" commented Biff.

"Headliners—right on the front page," came from Chet.

"Well, they deserve it, don't they?" put in another high school student.

"They certainly do," answered Chet.

"And to think Jack Dodd and his dad are cleared," went on Biff. "That's the best yet."

"Jack's smiling like a basket of chips," said Tony. "Mouth all on a broad grin."

So the talk ran on among the boys.

The girls were equally enthusiastic.

"Oh, I think Frank and Joe are too wonderful for anything," remarked Callie Shaw, who had always been looked on with favor by Frank.

"I never thought Joe could be so brave," breathed Iola Morton.

"They are sure a pair of heroes," said Paula Robinson.

"I really think they ought to be in a book," added Tessie, her twin.

Even the Applegates, for whom the Hardy boys had solved the mystery of the tower treasure, had their word of commendation.

"As brave as the knights of old," said Miss Adelia.

"If I had my say, I'd print a stamp in their honor," said Hurd Applegate, who was an expert on stamp collecting.

The new roadster became famous in Bayport as the car that had lured the auto thieves to their downfall. Motorists in general were able to breathe easier when they learned that the gang had been rounded up. A little to their embarrassment and much to their delight, at a banquet of the Automobile Club, Frank and Joe were the guests of honor.

"I am sure," said the president of the club, in a speech, "that the automobile owners of the city are grateful to these two boys for the courage and ingenuity they displayed in running down the gang when even the organized police had failed. They ran grave risks, for they were dealing with desperate and experienced criminals. If the hiding place had not been discovered, it seems likely that the thefts might have continued for some time and it is certain that none of the cars would have been recovered. As it is, all the automobiles have been located and returned to their owners, as well as all the stolen goods. As you all know, various rewards were offered by this association and by a number of the car owners, and to these rewards the Hardy boys are justly entitled. I have great pleasure, then, in presenting them with the sum of fifteen hundred dollars, comprising the three separate rewards of five hundred dollars each."

Amid cheers, two checks for $750 were presented to Frank and Joe.

Mr. Hardy, who was present at the banquet, beamed with pleasure. But when he returned home with the lads he invited them into his study and closed the door. Wondering what was coming, the boys faced their father.

"I think you've had enough congratulations for one week," he said to his sons. "Don't let it turn your heads."

"We won't, Dad," they promised.

"It was a good idea, hiding in that locker," their father remarked. "It was a good idea and it worked out very well. There was only one thing wrong with it."

"What was that?" asked Frank.

"It was too dangerous."

"Too dangerous?"

"You took too many chances, dealing with a gang like that. Don't try anything like that again or I may have to hunt up my old shaving strop."

But Fenton Hardy smiled indulgently as he spoke.

"He wasn't real mad," whispered Joe, as he and his brother left their father. "He was only a little bit provoked."

"Well, it really was dangerous—hiding in that locker," admitted Frank. "Those thieves might have caught us like rats in a trap."

"I wonder if we'll have any more such thrilling adventures," mused Joe.

Additional thrilling adventures were still in store for the brothers, and what some of them were will be related in another volume, to be entitled, "The Hardy Boys: The Secret of the Caves."

In that volume we shall meet all our old friends again and learn how a peculiar accident led up to a most unlooked-for climax.

The reception Frank and Joe received at the Automobile Club was tame in comparison to the way they were greeted by their chums.

"The biggest little detectives in the world," was the way Chet expressed himself.

"They can't be beat!" came from Tony Prito.

"But it's nothing to what I expect them to do in the future," was Biff Hooper's comment.

Made in the USA
Las Vegas, NV
17 December 2024